The
Shadow Collector's
Apprentice

The Shadow Collector's Apprentice

AMY GORDON

Holiday House / New York

Library of Congress Cataloging-in-Publication Data

Gordon, Amy, 1949-

The shadow collector's apprentice / by Amy Gordon. — 1st ed.

p. cm.

Summary: In the summer of 1963, after his father has inexplicably disappeared
leaving Cully with his three eccentric aunts on their barely profitable apple farm,
Cully goes to work for a mysterious antiques dealer who has the strange
hobby of collecting shadows.

ISBN 978-0-8234-2359-0 (hardcover)

[1. Shadows—Fiction.   2. Magic—Fiction.   3. Aunts—Fiction.   4. Moths—Fiction.
5. Fathers and sons—Fiction.]   I. Title.

PZ7.G65Sh 2012

[Fic]—dc22

2011007271

For Weezie

June 14, 1963

For the hundredth time, I'm wondering why Jack ran off.

The maple tree he loved in the front yard looks dead. It's the only tree on the property that doesn't have leaves. It shed them a year ago in the fall, not leaf by leaf like other maples, but like a ginkgo tree, all at once, and not a single leaf has come back this spring. I believe it's grieving for Jack. It always *was* his special tree.

I guess I'm thinking about it so much because today is Cully's birthday. Twelve years old, and the poor boy has no mother, his father is who-knows-where, and he's stuck living in this house with three old aunts. (Well, I guess we aren't that old—not one of us is a day over forty.)

We know Jack is more or less okay because every now and then a postcard arrives from him. He's been working and living on farms all over the world, but he never says how he really is or when he's coming home.

All we know is that one cold morning in January, Cully woke up to find that awful note:

I love you, son, with all my heart, but I have to go and seek my fortune. If all goes well, I'll be home soon. I know the aunts will take good care of you as they have always done.

Well, maybe we shouldn't have been so surprised— Jack was not himself in those days before he took off. I know he was worried about the farm and how we were going to manage, but he was acting mighty strange—for one thing, he was sneaking Pennyacre antiques over to Batty's Attic for extra cash.

Oooh—just writing about it makes me want to cry. Miggs and Opal are mad at him, but I'm just plain sad and worried. I know Jack loves Cully and the farm too much to *want* to leave us. I think something terrible has happened to him, and I think it might have something to do with— ooh—I better not even write it down. Jack would not like me to...

It makes me shiver even thinking about it.

But now I have to get back to work on my moth and myth book. When I think of the books I have written and illustrated, this is my favorite. I love drawing moths— they are so fluttery and mysterious and interesting—what Tennyson called "the filmy shapes that haunt the dusk." So many moths are named after people or creatures in myths. *Myths and Moths* looks good as a title, but it's hard to say, a bit like trying to talk with peanut butter stuck to the roof of your mouth. *Moths and Myths*? Better. Or what about—*Mothology*?

1

"Here's something," said Cully Pennyacre, pointing to an ad in the *Medley Monitor*. Seeking apprentice. 12-16 yrs. old. Batty's Attic.

Cully and Sam Cleary sat in a booth drinking root-beer floats at Pete's Parlor on Main Street. They were celebrating Cully's birthday and the beginning of summer vacation, and Cully was looking in the paper for a job because Aunt Opal had said she couldn't afford to give him an allowance anymore.

"Let me see that," said Sam, reaching for the paper. "Don't you usually have to be sixteen or older for most jobs?" And then he said, "Shh, don't look up—Archie just walked in."

Until recently, Archie Sticks had been a good buddy of theirs, but overnight he had changed from being an easygoing kid to picking fights with everyone. During basketball practice one afternoon he socked Sam in the face for no apparent reason. Two days later he punched another boy. Coach Stevens kicked him off the team. At school he turned over his desk when he couldn't answer a question in math class. The principal called in Archie's parents, but they said he was just as bad at home and they didn't understand it at all.

No one knew what was eating Archie Sticks.

"Hey," said Archie, standing beside their booth.

"Hey," said Sam, not very enthusiastically.

"You're not applying for *that*, are you?" he asked. He stabbed at the ad in the newspaper. "I tried it. Turned out to be real dumb."

"No harm in checking it out," said Cully.

"The job doesn't even pay," said Archie.

Cully and Sam didn't invite Archie to sit down with them, so Archie stood awkwardly beside the booth until he finally said, "Well, see ya around. I get the hint—I can tell when three's a crowd."

Cully and Sam sighed as Archie slouched off.

"I used to like that kid, but now I can't wait to see the back of him," said Sam.

"Yeah," Cully agreed, "and now I'm definitely going to check out the apprentice job at Batty's. If Archie didn't like it, it must be great."

"No kidding!" said Sam with a laugh.

As Cully put the paper down, Sam pointed to the headline. "Look at this—'Spy in London caught trying to get secrets from former War Minister.'"

"It's all because of the Cold War," said Cully.

"I don't get this Cold War stuff," said Sam. "How can a war be cold?"

"We're not fighting the Soviet Union directly, so it's not a hot war," said Cully. "We don't have our army shooting at their army. Instead we just spy on each other, and put up a wall in Berlin to keep the east and west apart, and have this big competition to see who can get to the moon first."

Sam shook his head in admiration. "How come you know so much?"

"My dad talks to me all the time about current events,"

Cully mumbled. Or *used* to talk to me, he should have said, but he didn't want Sam asking questions about his father, like what was he doing and when was he coming back. Cully didn't want to admit he didn't know.

The boys slipped out of the booth, and as they stepped outside Cully said, "Come over tomorrow and we'll go fishing."

"Sounds good to me," said Sam, and punching Cully lightly on the arm, he went in one direction and Cully in the other.

Batty's Attic was around the corner from the bookstore, down an alley next to a thrift shop and a vacuum repair shop. BATTY'S ATTIC, the sign said. Antiques-Furniture-Books-Valuables-Gold and Silver-Bought, Sold, Appraised/ Loans-Good Prices.

As Cully went in, the door jangled and a white dog lying curled up in the corner lifted its head and thumped its tail. Cully reached down and patted it.

"Hello, there, can I help you?" Jim Bates, commonly known as Batty, was sitting up on a stool behind a glass case at one end of the store. He was a round man with white hair sparsely decorating the dome of his head, and he was wearing a pair of round glasses.

Cully took in the jumble all around him. There were old chairs, bookshelves crammed with ancient-looking books, bureaus cluttered with lamps and vases.

"Something in particular you're looking for?" Batty asked.

"I'm, er, applying for the job—the, er, apprentice job," said Cully.

"Ah, the apprentice job—wonderful!" Batty said enthusiastically. He peered at Cully. Behind his glasses, his eyes were oddly blurry, as if they didn't focus quite right. "What age might you be?"

"Today is my birthday," said Cully. "I'm turning twelve. The ad said you're looking for twelve- to sixteen-year-olds."

Batty smiled cheerfully, but it was a rather goofy smile because one of his front teeth was broken. "Well, then, felicitations on the anniversary of your birth, and to celebrate perhaps you could indulge me in a little hobby. I collect shadows, and I'd love to collect yours. I'll just bet you have a fine, dark one."

Cully stared at Batty. "You collect *shadows*?"

"Please come back to my studio, and I will show you." Batty climbed down from his stool and opened a door behind him. Cully had to step around a pile of catalogs to get behind the counter. He followed Batty through the door and down a dark hall. The white dog padded after them.

"Good boy, Fitz," said Batty, talking to the dog as he unlocked another door. "And now," he said, turning on the light, "you see before you my pride and joy, my shadow-maker." He pointed to a large camera-like apparatus that stood in the middle of the large room.

Cully thought the room smelled just like Aunt Inca's darkroom at the farmhouse where she developed photographs by dunking film into a basin of chemicals. Cully always liked watching the pictures emerge, and then when an image was ready to be "fixed," Inca would dunk it into a different basin.

"If you would just go over and stand on that large X," said Batty, pointing again.

Cully hesitated. "I don't understand. You're going to—*make* my shadow?"

"Oh my," said Batty, shaking his head. "You're the kind who needs to understand! Well, you don't need to understand everything just yet. Do go over and stand on that X, and soon all will be revealed."

"I don't want to be zapped with something weird," said Cully. "You won't turn me into a zombie, will you?"

Batty laughed. "The modern child watches too many movies. Now, let's see, how about I zap old Fitz here first to reassure you? Oh my, did I say zap? I meant to say, let's apply electromagnetic radiation of a certain wavelength." Batty turned off the overhead light and flicked a switch on the apparatus. A beam of light was projected onto one of the walls.

"Go on, Fitz, stand over there, boy!" Batty pulled a biscuit from his pocket and tossed it onto the X. As Fitz walked eagerly over to the spot, a doggy shadow sprang up on the wall. The shadow tail wagged just as vigorously as the real one, but as Fitz finished the treat and moved out of the light, the shadow remained frozen on the wall. Cully's mouth dropped open.

"Is it magic?"

Batty laughed slightly. "Enchanting, isn't it?" he asked. "Do let me elucidate: the wall is painted with a special paint that absorbs photons. They hold onto light, so even after Fitz isn't standing there blocking the light anymore, thereby creating the shadow, it *seems* as if the shadow is still there."

"Oh," said Cully, surprised by the explanation. It really had seemed like magic.

"And then I apply a fixative to preserve the shadow, because the paint won't hold onto the light indefinitely, of course." Batty carried a basin of chemicals over to the wall, dipped a paintbrush in, and slapped the stuff onto Fitz's shadow. The smell of chemicals stung Cully's nose. "Just turn on that timer, will you?" Batty asked, nodding in the direction of the counter. "Seven seconds is enough for a dog shadow. Humans take a bit longer."

"Are dog and human shadows different?" Cully asked as he turned the pointer on the dial.

Batty pulled a pair of tweezers from his pocket. "Oh yes," he said. "If you become my apprentice, that's just one of many entrancing things you'll learn."

At the "ding," Batty gripped one of Fitz's shadow ears with the tweezers. "Easy does it," he said, pulling gently. Soon the entire shadow peeled off the wall. It looked like a piece of dirty laundry as Batty held it up. The blank wall now shone almost too brightly.

Fitz suddenly lay down with a groan.

"Oh gosh, taking his shadow—did it hurt him?" Cully asked with alarm.

Batty laughed. "What an extraordinary idea! A boy with an imagination!" Batty bent down and gave Fitz a hearty pat. "You're all right, aren't you, Fitz? But in any case," he added, straightening up, "I'm not in the business of collecting dog shadows." He carried the shadow over to a sink and ran it under a faucet, and the shadow seemed to dissolve. Fitz scrambled to his feet, shaking himself all over as if he'd been swimming. He padded over to Cully and pressed against him.

"Good dog," said Cully, patting him. He seemed fine now, and his shadow, just beneath him on the floor, seemed fine, too.

"Now, dear boy, do say I may collect your shadow." Batty raised his eyebrows in anticipation.

A cautious place in Cully still niggled, but curiosity got the better of him. Fitz, after all, did seem just fine. "Okay," he said.

Batty turned on the light. "Go ahead, have fun. Lunge, leap, lollop," he said encouragingly.

Standing in the light, Cully felt a slight fizzing sensation all over, as if he'd been dunked in bubbly tonic water. He jumped as high as he could, and then laughed as he stepped out of the light and saw his shadow still jumping.

"Now, then," said Batty. He painted Cully's shadow with chemicals. "Set the timer for twelve seconds...and here we go," he added cheerfully as the timer went off. "I always like to start at the top—" He stopped. The tweezers kept slipping, not gripping the shadow at all. "Ha!" he exclaimed. "Ha! Well, look at that! Doesn't want to separate!"

"Separate?"

"From the, er, wall." Batty looked at Cully curiously. "Are you *sure* it's your birthday today?"

"Of course I'm sure," said Cully.

"Well, well!" Batty exclaimed again, his round face beaming with excitement. "Tell me your name, boy!"

"Cully Pennyacre."

Batty looked at him in astonishment. "Oh my goodness! Pennyacre! Of course, I should have known. You are a living image of your father—a youthful version, with that same head of strawberry blond hair. He's—uh—I believe he's—"

"He had to travel somewhere," said Cully, turning red. Sometimes he hated living in a small town where everyone knew everyone else's business.

"Yes, of course," said Batty kindly. "I'm so sorry I brought it up. Let's change the subject, shall we? I'm fairly certain you're in my granddaughter's class at school—her name is Isabel Ballou."

Cully nodded. He knew Isabel, all right. The only new girl in the sixth-grade class, Isabel had unfortunately rubbed kids the wrong way almost immediately.

"She talks about you, you know," said Batty. "I gather you are actually cordial to her. Her other classmates, I believe, are a churlish lot."

Cully squirmed uncomfortably. He didn't think he was *that* nice to Isabel—he just wasn't mean the way a lot of the other kids were.

Batty fixed Cully with his strange, unfocused gaze. "Hmm, yes, you're a popular boy, by all accounts. And I've heard you're a whiz on the middle-school basketball team."

"I like to play," said Cully, who didn't like to brag.

"No, no, please, just allow me to brood on the facts at hand—hmm, let's see—yes, your mother—I'm so sorry—I believe she passed away several years ago, yes?"

Cully frowned, looking at the floor. He wondered if Jim Bates had grilled Archie like this—if so, no wonder Archie hadn't wanted the job.

"Ah, didn't mean to pry," said Batty, as if reading Cully's thoughts, "but your circumstances go a long way toward explaining things. What a sensational apprentice you will make!"

Cully kept one hand on Fitz's head—Batty was making him nervous, and having the dog close by was reassuring.

Batty opened his mouth and seemed about to explain, but then he changed his mind. "Let's return to the front of the store, shall we? Don't like to leave the few valuables I have out there unattended for too long."

Batty turned off the light and locked the door, and Cully followed him down the hall. "Um, Mr. Bates," Cully said as he stepped past the counter into the storefront, "what exactly happened in there with my shadow?"

"You must call me Batty," said Batty, smiling his broken-toothed smile as he sat down on his stool. Fitz went over to his corner and lay down. "And that, my boy, is the wrong question. You ought to be asking what your duties as an apprentice will be. And my answer: help me collect shadows, attend to the stock, and so forth. I will instruct you in the finer mysteries as time goes on."

"I really need to get a job that pays," said Cully cautiously.

"You *will* get paid," said Batty. "Far better wages than anyone else your age. You simply start off with your efforts freely given—just to make sure we're both happy. Cogitate upon it tonight, Cully. Then tomorrow at this time I shall see you again, if you are so inclined."

The door jangled open. Isabel Ballou came into the store. She was wearing a pink top and pink shorts. Her mousy brown hair was pulled back by a pink hair-band. She was definitely what Aunt Miggs called a "girly-girl."

"Hi, Grandpa," she said.

Fitz's tail thumped happily, but Batty made a face. "Oh," he said, not very nicely, "it's you. I thought I told you I didn't want you hanging about the store anymore."

"I'm walking Fitz," Isabel said, her lower lip trembling slightly. "Remember, that's the one job you're allowing me to do."

"Not for long, if all goes well," said Batty. "You know Cully Pennyacre, don't you?"

"Oh yes, of course, *Cully*," Isabel said, darting a sideways glance at Cully. "I beat him on the geography test at the end of the year by three points."

"Such a smarty-pants," said Batty with a sigh.

Kids didn't like Isabel Ballou, Cully thought, because she was always showing off, using big words, bragging about her grades. Now she reached up for a leash that was hanging on the wall and clipped it to Fitz's collar. "Come on, Fitzy-Fitz, time for your constitutional," she said.

As Isabel headed out of the store, she almost ran into her mother, Kipper Ballou, who was on her way in. "What are you doing with that dog, Isabel?" she asked sharply. "You're going to be late for your lesson."

"No, I'm not," said Isabel, tossing her head. "I never am."

Isabel marched off, and Kipper stepped all the way in, filling every inch and corner of the store with the strong scent of perfume. She was a relatively new real-estate agent in Medley—very different, Cully's aunts said, from Cindy Rogers, the realtor who had been in town for years. For one thing, Kipper always wore high heels and expensive-looking suits.

"Hello, Pops." Kipper turned to Batty and smiled at him with a lipsticky smile. "I have a new customer for you."

"And I have some good news for *you!*" said Batty. He stepped out from behind the counter, rubbing his hands together. "This is Cully Pennyacre, my new apprentice," he said, standing beside Cully and putting a hand on his shoulder. "Well, he isn't *yet*, but I hope he will be."

Kipper eyed Cully. "I still don't understand why Isabel can't work for you, Pops. We should be keeping the business in the family—at least, that's what Bobo says—he says it's a big mistake, and—"

"She's too young, and that's that," Batty snapped.

"Well, all right, no need to bite my head off," said Kipper mournfully. She shook her head and even more perfume filled the air. "So—Cully Pennyacre—kind of a coincidence seeing you here. I was thinking of stopping by the farm and paying your aunts a visit tonight."

"That's nice," said Cully, wondering why on earth Kipper would stop by. As far as he knew, she and his aunts hardly knew each other, but now the small storefront was filled with so much perfume he wanted desperately to escape. "I'll be heading out," he said. "Thanks, Mr. Bates, for, er, showing me around."

"Do call me Batty, and I shall see you tomorrow, dear boy," said Batty. "Shall I not?"

Cully didn't answer, and as he rode home on his bike his mind was swirling. Shadow-collecting was definitely a strange hobby. Batty was strange, too, with his flowery way of speaking. More than that, one moment he seemed nice and the next minute he was mean and grumpy—especially to his own granddaughter. Cully decided he wouldn't work for him.

Arriving home, Cully left his bike in the shed and then ran out into the orchard and lay down on his back and breathed in deeply. No more school for three whole months, he thought happily.

Shutting his eyes, he could hear the apple trees growing. The sound was difficult to describe, a bit like the humming of bees. It reminded him of the ongoing argument between the aunts: Miggs, the middle sister, had read a book by a lady named Rachel Carson. Pesticides, Miggs learned, could harm bees. Inca, the youngest, had read the book, too, and agreed. Both Miggs and Inca said they ought to stop using pesticides in the orchard. Opal, the eldest, said not to be silly—they couldn't grow healthy apples without something to kill the pests.

Cully sat up, stabbed through with pain at the idea of no more bees. Without bees to pollinate the blossoms, how could apple trees bear fruit?

He looked around at the orchard, at the pruned and well-cared-for trees. In the fall they produced a bounty of round, luscious apples. No matter how old he got, Cully was always a little surprised by their appearance. Where had they come from? Baldwins, Honeycrisps, Spencers, Early Macs, Paula Reds, Northern Spies, Golden Delicious, Macouns, Cortlands. The names, like the apples themselves, had a sort of magic to them.

"Let there be bees," he said out loud. The words sounded funny and made him laugh. He stood and began climbing the hill. The family's golden retrievers, Shep and Sheba, appeared and loped up the hill with him. At the top, a tall pine tree stood behind a ring of boulders, placed there to honor those who had once lived on Pennyacre Farm.

Cully stood before his grandparents' boulder. They had died within a few months of each other when he was seven. He had nothing but happy memories of Grandma Maisie, who had taught him how to identify birds, and of Grandpa Will, who had taught him how to make cider; and further-more, neither of his grandparents had *ever* spoken to him the way Batty spoke to Isabel.

Next Cully patted the boulder belonging to Melvin, Opal's husband. A few years back Melvin had been killed in a tragic train wreck. It had been sad for everyone—he had been such a nice guy, a good friend to Jack, a big help on the farm when he wasn't working at the lumber mill—but Opal, of course, had taken it the hardest. She hardly ever laughed anymore the way she used to.

And finally Cully knelt before his mother's boulder. He had been five when his mother died after a long illness. The aunts had taken over mothering him, each offering him something unique and wonderful, and he felt very grateful; still, he liked coming up here to the top of the hill and spending time with his mother's spirit. He ran his fingers over the raised letters of the plaque: **Tabitha Mayhew Pennyacre 1925–1957.**

"It's my birthday, Mom," he said out loud. "And everything's going okay except for Dad not being here."

And then he ran down the hill as fast as he could, filling his lungs with Pennyacre Apple Farm air.

At the bottom Cully found Miggs standing in the yard looking at the house, already changed out of her teaching clothes and wearing overalls. She was the science teacher at his school, but at home she was chief farmer and handywoman. With her tendency to wear overalls and her short, straight, brown hair cut square across her forehead, Cully always thought Miggs looked exactly like an older version of Scout in the movie *To Kill a Mockingbird*.

"No more teaching togs for a whole summer," Miggs said, smiling. "But now everywhere I turn I see all the things that have to be done. For one thing, the house needs repainting. Your father was the last one to paint it. Where'd he go, anyway?"

"You know where he went, Miggs," said Cully with a sigh. "He went to seek his fortune."

"Ah yes, his *fortune*," Miggs said, a scornful note in her voice.

"I can paint the house," Cully said quickly, hoping to prevent Miggs from saying anything more. Today, on his birthday, he didn't want to hear one single bad thing about his father.

"Well, that's dandy," said Miggs lightly. "Thank you very much for the offer. Now go and get washed up for your birthday dinner."

Up until Jack's departure Cully had lived with his father on the property in a small cottage nicknamed the "Chicken Coop." Now he lived in the big, old house, where, ever since his grandparents' death, Opal lived on the first floor, Miggs in the middle, and Inca on top. So far Cully had lived four months with Inca, and now he was living with Miggs; come September he'd move in with Opal—that is, if Jack hadn't returned by then.

As he headed toward the house Cully recognized the twinge in the pit of his stomach, the place that ached when he thought about his father.

2

For Cully's birthday everyone gathered downstairs in the big, old, original kitchen. Opal fired up the magnificent black cast-iron cookstove and made Cully his favorite meal. It felt good, he thought, for them all to be sitting around the old oak table, the hand-hewn beams above them, eating steak and baked potatoes and fresh asparagus from the garden. Opal also made her famous apple-rhubarb birthday pie and decorated it with twelve plus one-to-grow-on candles.

Cully scraped up the last bit of pie on his plate with his fork and let the taste linger on his tongue before washing it down with apple cider.

"Look at Cully, turning a year older right in front of our eyes," said Inca. Her long, copper-colored hair set off her blue eyes. Her whole look was warm and glowing.

Opal smiled. Her hair had a lot of white in it, and her face, usually drawn and pale, was slightly flushed with excitement.

"And now," said Miggs, jumping up from the table, "it's time for the presents!" She carried an armful of colorfully wrapped packages over to him.

Miggs's present was a new pair of overalls. "For painting in," she said. Opal gave him a new pair of socks. The beautiful wood-block print of a Polyphemus moth was from Inca.

"And there's one more," said Inca. "Guess who didn't forget your birthday?"

Cully's heart leaped as Inca handed him a postcard. On one side there was a picture of women in colorful kimono-like robes and scarves on their heads amid a clump of bushy trees. On the other side bright stamps decorated one corner, and his father's familiar scrawl covered the remaining space. *Happy Birthday, old man! Here are Japanese workers picking mulberry leaves for silkworms. I know Inca would like to see this. Also learning about Japanese beekeeping. All my love, Dad.* This was the fourth postcard Cully had received from Jack, each one from a different country.

"Last postcard he was working in an apple orchard in Wales," said Opal.

"He could be working in our own apple orchard right here," Miggs grumbled.

"Let's go out on the porch and enjoy the fireflies and eat another piece of Cully's birthday pie out there," said Inca, patting Cully's shoulder.

They were just settling on the porch, the three sisters in their rockers, Cully on the swing seat, when a sporty red convertible spun into the driveway and came to a screeching halt. Shep and Sheba, lying on the porch, scrambled to their feet and started barking.

"Yoo-hoo!" Kipper Ballou cried as she climbed out of the car. "Anybody home? I was just passing and I thought I'd drop by—hope I'm not disturbing you." Kipper came up the rickety porch stairs in her high heels and looked around. "These dogs don't bite, do they?" she asked nervously, as Sheba's bark turned into a low growl and the hackles rose on Shep's back.

"Not usually," said Miggs, getting a firm hold on Sheba's collar. "Whoa, dogs, what's going on with you? Shep, Sheba, sit down now and be quiet!"

Shep and Sheba sat and were quiet, and Kipper took a deep breath as she looked around. "Hello again—Cully, is it? Pops is looking forward to you working for him." Cully was about to say he hadn't definitely signed up for the job, but Kipper was off on another topic. "Lovely old place you've got here. And so much *land*." She stood by the porch railing, looking out. "But my goodness, there is a *lot* for you three gals to handle living here alone." She tugged at the front of her suit jacket, which was just a little too small for her. "With so much property, you could afford to develop some of it. That hill behind the orchard—must be nice views from up there."

"It's not—" Miggs started to say, but Kipper interrupted. "Oh, and just smell that pie! Delicious! Well, nice seeing you gals. Got to be going." She tottered down the stairs, her heels catching in a soft piece of old wood. She left a cloying cloud of perfume in her wake.

The two dogs threw themselves off the porch and raced down the stairs after her, barking their heads off as the red convertible squealed out of the driveway.

"She has some nerve!" Miggs exploded.

"Shep and Sheba think so, too," said Inca as the dogs lolloped back up the stairs and collapsed on the porch floor. "They're good watchdogs. Only bark at the people we don't like. Oh, and don't you just *hate* that word *gals*? Makes me think of old ladies in flowery hats eating pastries in coffee shops."

There was silence on the porch until Opal suddenly

cleared her throat. "Inca, I've been thinking. Maybe it's time for you to get a real job."

"Opalescence!" said Inca, shocked.

Opal's forehead was furrowed with worry. "It's just that—we're a little stretched for money right now."

"Inca *does* have a real job," said Miggs. "She makes beautiful books, and they do, by the way, bring in scads of money."

Opal sighed. "Book writing is like farming—you just never know from year to year what's going to happen."

"I was going to call my book *Mothology*," said Inca, staring out beyond the porch railing. "But perhaps Opal is right," she added sadly.

"You can't quit your book in the middle of writing it," said Miggs firmly. "Now listen, Opal, it's not as if Inca doesn't pull her weight around here—she's the one who stands behind the counter with the apple cider and apple butter every fall, and she sells more than we ever could because—well, because she's Inca, and everyone who sees her falls in love with her."

Opal actually smiled. Inca had many admirers, even if they were *feckless*, as Opal liked to call them.

The mood on the porch lifted, and Inca said, "Look at the fireflies, will you? I don't think I've ever seen so many." Here, there, everywhere, lights blinked, winked, and danced. "Fireflies are called *Lampyridae* in Latin. A chemical reaction in the abdomen of the firefly produces the light. It's called bioluminescence. And do you know what, Cully? I think they're sending you a message. Like in Morse code. They're saying, Happy Birthday to you, dear Cully, Happy Birthday to you." Inca's light voice broke into song.

Watching, Cully could easily believe the bugs were flashing him a silent birthday greeting. With his father's postcard in his pocket and summer vacation stretching before him, he would have felt truly content except for the worry about money that seemed to linger in the air. It clung to everything, like Kipper Ballou's perfume. Cully resolved then and there to go back to Batty's Attic and work long enough as an apprentice to get paid.

3

On the first day of summer vacation, Cully was lying in the four-poster bed his dad had slept in as a boy. He stared for a moment at Jack's old baseball trophies, but then it was time to get up and start scraping the peeling paint off the side of the house before the sun got too high and made it sweltering up there on the ladder.

Cully pulled on the birthday overalls, tucked his father's postcard into his pocket, and went out to the second-floor kitchen.

Miggs had set out a bowl of cereal for him. She'd probably been up for hours. Cully heard the gurgling of water in the pipes down below. Opal was doing laundry, her Saturday morning chore. During the week she handled the accounts at the lumber company. Above him on the top floor, Inca played records of Frank Sinatra as she worked on her book. Maybe she didn't have a "real" job, but she never stopped working, even on weekends. Cully gobbled some cereal, ran down the back stairs that ended in the mudroom, and went outside.

Miggs had already placed a ladder for him against the house and a set of scrapers at the bottom. She was up on another ladder. Cully climbed up and the two of them scraped in companionable silence all morning.

"You keep at things, Cully," Miggs said finally. "I don't know many other boys your age who would stick to something as boring as this. Let's have lunch."

Miggs brought lunch out to the porch. Along the edge of the railing the lilacs were just past, their blossoms little, crumbly things. Red roses were growing up the trellis. A bee drifted up onto the porch.

"Hey! There's a bee," said Cully. "The pesticides haven't gotten them yet."

"Not yet," said Miggs, frowning slightly, "but we *have* to stop using poison. Mr. Masumoto at the gardening center says his son Kento is in Japan right now learning about natural ways to get rid of pests. He'll be able to teach us when he gets back."

"I wonder if Kento will run into Dad," said Cully, pulling out the postcard.

"Let's hope he does, and let's hope he brings Jack home," said Miggs. She took a decisive bite out of her sandwich.

Opal, who had been pegging up sheets on the line outside, came up to the porch. She sighed heavily as she sat down in her rocking chair.

"Have a sandwich and some lemonade, Ope," said Miggs. "We have extra, and you ought to be eating more. You're looking thin these days."

"That's a mighty nice compliment, Miggs," said Opal with a slight smile, "and I will, thank you. You're working for that Jim Bates, are you, Cully?"

"I meant to tell you yesterday, Opal," Cully said. "I'm gonna go and work just a few hours in the afternoons."

"What are you doing for him?" she asked.

23

"This and that," said Cully vaguely. *Collecting shadows* sounded too weird.

"Don't know that much about him—he hasn't been in town that long," said Opal.

"Moved here about the same time as that Kipper Ballou," said Miggs.

"She's his daughter," said Cully. "She came into the store yesterday."

"Well," said Opal, wrinkling her nose, "I hope he's nicer than she is, or that banker husband of hers. As far as I can tell, he's a little eccentric but harmless. Jack spent quite a bit of time doing odd jobs for him before he—before he—" Opal broke off in midsentence. She hated talking about Jack. She sat up and cleared her throat. "Is Jim Bates paying you?"

"He says he will, just not at first."

"I'm awful sorry about your allowance," she said. "It's just that right now we have to be very careful."

Cully stood and put his plate and glass on the lunch tray. "I'm going to go and mow the grass in the orchard now," he said. The drawn look on Opal's face was making him uneasy. He thought of how every evening for the past couple of months he'd seen her sitting at the roll-top desk in a corner of her kitchen, bills piled up in front of her.

Cully soon forgot to worry as he rode the tractor up and down between the long rows of trees. He knew that keeping the grass short kept the pests away, and besides, the orchard looked better trim and neat, and the cut grass smelled so good. He made sure to keep the clover beneath the trees to attract the bees, and here and there he saved a cluster of buttercups from the chopping blades.

"Go on and do something fun now, Cully," said Miggs when he had finished. "You can't be working all the time."

"I think I'll just poke around in the Chicken Coop for a while," he said.

"Not going to find what he wants in there," said Miggs under her breath. "Gone to seek his fortune, indeed! His fortune is right here with that son of his—fortuneate he was, and didn't even know it." Cully wasn't sure if she meant him to overhear her or not; of the three sisters, Miggs was the maddest at Jack.

The door of the Chicken Coop was swollen from dampness. Cully had to yank at it to get it open. The place smelled musty. Mouse droppings littered the floor, and the curtains, once a bright, cheerful yellow, were fading.

Cully didn't know what he was looking for, really, but from time to time he liked coming into the Coop, as if he could, just by breathing the air, recapture the past when his mother was still alive, when his dad was still at home. Going into his parents' bedroom he was, as usual, drawn to the dresser where the framed photograph of Jack and Tabitha still sat. There they were, arm in arm, looking happy. He could have brought the photograph into the big house with him, but he felt it belonged right where it was.

The children's books his mother had written were still lined up on top of the dresser. He pulled out *The ABC'S of PENNYACRE APPLE FARM* and leafed through it. "A... apple aroma when the cider is evaporating...B...Baldwin apples and blue jays...C...cinnamon in applesauce..." Grandma Maisie had read the book over and over to him when he was small.

Replacing the book, Cully tried to pull open the top

drawer. It was swollen shut, and he yanked a bit too hard and fell backward with the entire drawer onto the bed. He sat up, laughing, and scooped up some of the contents that had come flying out—a few pairs of socks, some pieces of paper, some pennies, a paper clip. One of the pieces of paper caught his eye. It was a yellow receipt.

BATTY'S ATTIC was printed at the top. Then in large block letters was written: *JANUARY 12, 1963, JACK PENNYACRE: 1 POCKET WATCH & 1 S.*

Cully frowned. He looked in the top drawer again, remembering that was where his father had always kept his great-grandfather Cullen's silver pocket watch. It wasn't there. So had his father sold the watch? And what was an S?

Realizing he needed to get a move on if he was going to get to Batty's Attic by two o'clock, Cully replaced the drawer, slipped the receipt into his pocket, and raced to get his bike.

"Ah, there you are! Sound the trumpets, beat the drums!" Batty exclaimed as Cully walked into the store. Fitz raised his head, thumping his tail. Once again Cully was struck by something out-of-focus about Batty. Batty's rejoicing was cut short as the door jangled open again. A tall man with a thatch of white hair came in, followed closely by Kipper Ballou.

"Oh hello, there," Kipper said as she saw Cully. "How is that gorgeous piece of Pennyacre property doing?" Without waiting for an answer she said, "Brought Mr. Crimps along with me today."

Mr. Crimps bent down to pat Fitz. "Nice dog you got there. I used to keep a dog. Going to get me another one—a nice old dog, just like me. Housebroken like me, too." He laughed a dry, old laugh. "He and I, we'll go for walks. I've been sittin' around too much."

"Mr. Crimps brought his antique books for you to look at, Pops," said Kipper.

Batty came out from behind the counter and walked over to a table at the back of the room with chairs arranged around it. "Ah, Mr. Crimps, I like nothing better than a bibliophile. Let's take a look, shall we?"

Mr. Crimps set down several fat, leather-bound books with gold lettering. "All by Mr. Charles Dickens. First editions," he said.

"Spectacular condition! My, my, such paragons, such pearls!" exclaimed Batty. He picked up one of the books. "Ah, the richness of the leather!"

"I wouldn't part with 'em," said Mr. Crimps, "but I have this dream, you see, of movin' to Maine and livin' in my own little cottage with my own dog."

"Lovely dream," said Kipper, wagging her head and sending perfume billowing into the air.

Mr. Crimps nodded, his eyes lighting up. "Been thinking about this step for a while, but didn't think I could afford it. But then I'm standing in line at the bank telling my neighbor all about it, and Mrs. Ballou is in line behind me; she pipes up and tells me Jim Bates at Batty's Attic will give me a very good price for any old antiques I might have. Naturally I thought of my books."

"As indeed I will," said Batty. "What you have here defies credulity, Mr. Crimps. I'll just write you a fine, big check."

Batty wrote the check and handed it to Mr. Crimps. "Oh my!" the old man gasped. "I didn't know how much these books were worth!" He reached out and patted one of them fondly. "Thought of 'em more as friends than anything else. Since my wife passed away, many an evening Mr. Charles Dickens has kept me company. But now I'm going back home to Maine with a dog by my side. The day you overheard me talking was my lucky day, Mrs. Ballou!"

"Now then—I wonder if you'd indulge me, Mr. Crimps," said Batty, scraping back his chair and standing. "I have a harmless, innocent, foolish little hobby—collecting shadows! I'd dearly love to collect yours."

"Shadow-collecting? Whatever do you mean?" asked Mr. Crimps.

"Come take a walk with me, O dear Mr. Crimps, come follow me," said Batty. "Cully, my boy, give me a hand. A perfect opportunity to initiate you in your duties as apprentice."

Cully followed Batty and Mr. Crimps down the hallway. As Batty unlocked the door he said, "Please, dear Mr. Crimps, stand on that X. And if you would be so kind as to turn on the shadow-maker, Cully, I'll prepare the fixative."

As Cully found the "on" button, the air filled with the smell of chemicals. Mr. Crimps, standing in the beam of light, chuckled slightly, rubbing his stomach. "It tickles," he said. He waved his arms and chuckled again. "Watch this. I learned this when I was knee-high to a grasshopper." Poking up two fingers of one hand, he made a rabbit shadow. Its long ears waggled and its nose twitched. With the fingers of his other hand he made blades of grass for the rabbit to nibble. "I can make a dog, too. Woof, woof!"

"All right, dear Mr. Crimps, do step away now, please," said Batty.

Mr. Crimps stepped away. His eyes grew large as he saw

his shadow frozen to the wall. "Look at that!" he exclaimed. "How'd ya do that?"

"Photons, Mr. Crimps," said Batty, "a little trick of science. In a sense I've taken a photograph of your shadow, and now I'm going to 'fix' it, just as they do in the camera shops. Perhaps, O apprentice of mine, I could get you to apply the chemicals."

Turning his head slightly away from the smell, Cully carried the basin of chemicals carefully over to the wall. Holding his breath, he dipped the paintbrush in and then swept the concoction across the shadow.

"Lovely," said Batty approvingly, "daub away, my boy. Now then, we turn on the timer. Twelve seconds."

Mr. Crimps shook his white head. "Can't for the life of me understand why anybody would have a hobby like that."

Batty was already standing at the wall, applying tweezers to the shadow. He started at the top.

"Well, I'll be!" said Mr. Crimps. "You see something new every—" He stopped talking abruptly as the last of the shadow came off the wall.

"Now then, Cully," said Batty. "If you'd lead Mr. Crimps back out to Mrs. Ballou."

Mr. Crimps seemed confused and disoriented. "This way, Mr. Crimps," said Cully, and taking him by the arm he led the old man out of the room and down the hall. "What kind of dog do you think you'll get?"

Mr. Crimps gazed at Cully with a troubled expression. "A dog at my age? What was I thinking? Have to walk the darn things."

Cully looked at him, puzzled. "But Mr. Crimps, you said you'd like a dog when you move to Maine."

Back out in the storefront, Mr. Crimps sank down in a chair. He rubbed a hand across his face. "Who said anything about moving? Too much trouble."

Kipper was still sitting at the table going through a fat folder of papers. "A move at your age is hard, isn't it, Mr. Crimps?" she asked gently. She looked at him thoughtfully for a moment. "You know, there is going to be a new place just outside of town—we're calling it Apple Blossom Acres—isn't that a lovely name? And we're putting up the cutest little inexpensive cottages on it. All designed for—well, people advanced in years, just like you. Everything will be taken care of—we'll mow the lawn and walk your dog. We'll even pack you up and *move* you, Mr. Crimps."

"Apple Blossom Acres," Mr. Crimps repeated dully. The light seemed to have left his eyes. "Not expensive, you say. Ha!"

"Why, Mr. Crimps," said Kipper, "you sold your books just now for a very good amount of money—you ought to be *more* than able to buy into Apple Blossom Acres. The cottages will *not* be expensive. People are signing up for them already, and they're going fast. I'd like to drive you by the property right now so you can get a feeling for it."

"All right," Mr. Crimps said, rising unsteadily to his feet. "Why not?"

"Where is Apple Blossom Acres going to be?" Cully asked.

"Oh, just outside of town," said Kipper airily. "Amazing how much farmland is for sale these days."

As Kipper swept Mr. Crimps out the door, Cully sank into a chair, feeling breathless. Something very strange had happened when Batty "collected" the old man's shadow.

As Batty came back through the door from the hallway, the front door jangled open and Fitz's tail began wagging a mile a minute. Isabel was wearing a pink dress and a pink ribbon in her hair. She looked like a neatly tied-up birthday package. "What are you doing here, Isabel?" Batty asked rudely.

Isabel sighed. "I'm here for Fitz." As she leaned down to pet the dog, Fitz looked up at her with adoring eyes.

"I've got someone else to walk Fitz now," Batty said, nodding toward Cully. "How about a frisk for Fitz, my boy?"

"I'm going to take Fitz," said Isabel, pouting. "You said it was *my* job."

"Oh honestly, if you want to go with him, then go!" Batty snapped. "Always a fuss about something!"

Isabel's face looked pinched for a moment. She picked up the leash. "You get the ball, Cully. He likes to chase it, but it's muculent and I don't like to touch it. Come on, Fitz, let's perambulate."

Cully looked about self-consciously as he walked down Main Street. Fitz stopped constantly to sniff at every little thing, and Cully wished they would hurry up and get to the woods. He didn't want to be seen by his friends with Isabel Ballou. They finally headed up a side street that led to the river.

In the woods Isabel let Fitz off the leash. Cully threw the ball for him.

"Are you really Grandpa's apprentice?" she asked. "I wanted that job."

"You couldn't be," said Cully. "You're not even twelve, I bet." Isabel had often announced to the class that she had skipped first grade.

"I don't see what the big deal about being twelve is. I

grew up in antique stores. Everywhere we lived, Grandpa had a store. I know how to tell if a bureau is old or if it's tricked to look old. I know how to tell a real gem from a fake. I would be a much better apprentice than anyone else."

"Why aren't you, then?"

"Because—because my grandfather doesn't want me to be because—I don't know why—because he's crabby like that sometimes."

Cully thought there was something else she wanted to say, but Fitz came bounding up and dropped the ball at Isabel's feet. Isabel shrank back. She was a skinny, frail little thing, Cully reflected. He gave the ball a kick.

"Oh no, Fitz is in the river!" Isabel wailed. "He's going to get all wet and dirty."

"Dogs are *supposed* to get dirty," said Cully. He picked up a stick and whacked at a dead branch poking out from a tree. It broke off with a satisfying crack. "What gives with all the shadow stuff, anyhow?" he asked.

Isabel turned away slightly. "It's Grandpa's weird hobby." She looked at her watch. "We should be getting back. I have a pottery lesson at three, flute at four, and sewing at five."

Cully looked at her curiously. "Don't you mind all those lessons?"

Isabel cocked her head to one side. "Swimming can be tiring. Here, Fitzy-Fitz," she called. She sagged a bit, looking discouraged. "He never comes when I call him."

Cully put two fingers in his mouth and whistled. As Fitz came bounding toward them, Isabel shrank back again. "How'd you do that?" she asked.

Cully whistled again, showing her just how he placed his fingers.

Isabel made a face. "I'm not going around sticking my fingers in my mouth."

"Try this, then." Cully picked up an acorn and popped off the cap with his thumb, and then, cupping it in his hands, blew across the top, making a piercing whistle. He handed it to her.

Isabel made a few halfhearted attempts at blowing and then dropped the cap into the pink purse she carried.

As Cully and Isabel were walking back up Main Street, Archie Sticks was coming toward them. As Archie passed by he purposely bumped hard into Cully.

"Whatcha doing?" asked Cully.

"Oh, so sorry, didn't see you there," said Archie. "Musta been I was blinded by Isabel's beauty." He kept on walking.

"What is the matter with him?" asked Cully, staring at Archie's back. "He never used to be such a jerk."

"Family troubles," said Isabel primly. "At least that's what Kipper says."

"Kipper?" Cully asked. "You mean your mother?"

"She's not my mother," said Isabel. "She's my aunt, and Kipper says Archie Sticks's father is a drunk."

"Well, good for Kipper," Cully mumbled, but he looked at Isabel differently. "Kipper is your *aunt*?"

"My parents died when I was little," said Isabel. "Kipper was my mom's sister. She and Bobo couldn't have kids, so they adopted me. Grandpa mostly takes care of me, because Kipper and Bobo are very busy."

Isabel spoke so matter-of-factly Cully felt there was nothing he could say, but he couldn't help feeling sympathetic. He knew what it was like not to have a mother—and at least for now, no father, either.

Isabel handed Cully the leash. "You take Fitz back. Grandpa and I just fight lately. We didn't use to. I don't know why we do now, all the time. It pretty much started when we moved to this boring old town." She paused. "Hey, thanks for letting me come with you—I mean, you hardly ever talk to me at school or anything."

Cully bit back something mean he might have said, and towed Fitz back into the store. As he came in Batty looked up from his perch behind the glass case. "Ah, there you are, a boy and a dog, back from the wonders of nature, and bravo, you seem to have lost my pesky granddaughter along the way."

Cully hung the leash up where it belonged and went over to the counter. "I was wondering why you were so surprised yesterday about my shadow not peeling off the wall. And today with Mr. Crimps—"

"Now, now, young man, no need to race your engine." Batty wagged a finger at Cully. "I like to give my apprentices a two-week trial period before I divulge too many secrets of the trade."

Cully sighed, wishing Batty would be more straightforward, but then his eye was caught by the jewelry on the shelves inside the glass case. There were bracelets, brooches, necklaces, watches, rings, and a little sign he hadn't noticed before. **Short on cash? Will keep your valuables for a reasonable amount of time. Good prices.**

The yellow receipt was still in his pocket; Cully drew it out. "People come here with watches and things and get a loan, right?" he asked.

"*Pawn* is the word I believe you are looking for," said Batty.

"I think you have my father's—or actually my great-grandfather's—watch." Cully held out the receipt.

"That's right, I do now recall the exact item." Batty stroked his chin thoughtfully. He reached into a drawer behind him. "This is the timepiece you are referring to?" He handed a silver watch to Cully.

"Yes," said Cully. He held the watch in the palm of one hand, loving the feel of the heavy silver. The initials C.A.P. were engraved on the cover. They stood for his namesake, Cullen Andrew Pennyacre. For a brief moment Cully was furious with his father for selling off a family heirloom, or pawning it; the watch was to have become his, Cully's, when he turned twenty-one. He reluctantly returned it to Batty.

"What does the S stand for?" he asked, showing Batty the receipt again.

"S," Batty echoed as he put the watch back in the drawer. He turned and patted down his few strands of white hair. "I fail to remember—oh, wait! It's coming back to me!" Batty smiled his broken-toothed smile. "S, dear boy, is for 'services rendered.' Should have been V.S.S. Very Special Services."

"What did he do?"

"Oh, this and that," said Batty vaguely. "Built me some shelves. Clever man, your father—a crackerjack was Jack—sorry he up and—disappeared."

"He's coming back," said Cully, anger flaring.

"Yes, of course he is," said Batty soothingly. "Tell you what, Cully. You work for me for two weeks—be vigilant, keep your beaming eyes wide open—but also keep your questioning mouth shut tight. At the end of a fortnight—that is two weeks, you know—I'll return the watch to you. How about it?"

"Okay," said Cully flatly.

"A first-class answer!" Batty exclaimed, punching the air with his fist. "That's just what I was hoping you'd say! Shop's closed tomorrow, but we shall meet again on Monday afternoon, dear boy, here amongst the fripperies and furbelows, the artifacts of bygone days. Having you on board cheers me up no end. For one thing, Isabel will not need to be here."

Cully wanted to ask why Batty wouldn't want her there, but the old man was ushering him out the door.

As Cully came out of the alley and onto Main Street, he was pleased to see Sam Cleary walking his bike toward him.

"Hey, I was just heading over to your place to go fishing," said Sam.

Riding down Route 5 toward Pennyacre Farm, Cully noticed the shadows of trees and telephone poles. They created a pattern in the road that set up a rhythm inside his head. Maybe there was an alternate world, Cully thought, a shadow world. Maybe Batty was populating the shadow world with his collection of shadows—or maybe more likely, he, Cully, was getting carried away.

Cully decided Sam Cleary was a good antidote to an overactive imagination. He was about as down-to-earth as a person could be. Together they dug at the edge of Miggs's vegetable garden and came up with half a dozen fat night crawlers.

But down at the river behind the house, at the widest part, where it was calm and still and the trout liked to bite, Cully started studying the reflections of the trees in the water. They were the opposite of shadows. They were there *because* of light, not because they were blocking light. The world they created in the river was an upside-down world. At that moment a fish bit. Cully reeled it in, and then Sam caught another a second later. The black flies were biting, too.

"Man, the bugs are wicked," said Sam, and, happy with their catch, the boys ran back to the house.

"Trout for supper," Cully said to Miggs.

"And asparagus from the garden," she said.

As the smell of butter and garlic filled the second floor, the phone rang.

"Hello," Miggs said, answering it. "Yes, he is. Just a moment, please. It's for you," Miggs said to Cully, handing him the phone.

Cully heard Isabel's slightly raspy voice. "Hi, Cully, listen to this." For a moment he didn't hear anything. Then there was a high-pitched whistling. "I can play Mozart on my acorn," she said.

"That's *Mozart*?" he asked. It didn't sound like any Mozart he had ever heard.

"I play the flute, you know—it wasn't all that hard to figure it out."

"Oh," he said. "Well." And then because there didn't seem to be anything else to say, he said, "Well, see ya later."

As he hung up the phone, Miggs was busy setting the table with her back to him. He could tell she was dying of curiosity. Much to his embarrassment, girls had been calling him all spring. Miggs tried to stay out of his business, but Sam didn't mind being nosey. "So who was that?" he asked.

"Just someone I showed how to whistle with an acorn," Cullyl said evasively.

"Neat-o," said Sam. "I can whistle between my teeth." He had a slight gap between his two front teeth, and he could whistle like a bird. He demonstrated and then went home to milk the cows on his family's dairy farm.

4

"I'm going to work in the garden until it gets dark," Miggs announced after supper.

Cully thought this was a perfect time to climb the stairs to Inca's floor and ask her some questions. Of the three sisters, she was the one most likely to talk to him about his father. Jack was only a year older than she was, and the two of them had always been close.

Coming into the Tower, as Inca's floor on the top was called, always seemed to Cully like climbing up into a tree house. There were lots of windows, and it was airy and filled with light. There were so many interesting things to look at, too—animal skulls and birds' nests on top of the bookshelves, art books on the shelves. Inca's drawings of insects were tacked up all over the walls. And Cully especially loved his great-grandfather Cullen's Chest of Moths. He could spend hours poring over it, pulling out the little drawers in which the moths were mounted, studying the incredible variety of their markings.

"Look at this," Inca said as Cully came into her little living room. She was curled up on a peppermint-striped couch with an old book in her lap. "*A Report on Insects Which Are Injurious to Vegetation*. Dated 1841. Lots of pests back then, but they picked 'em off by hand. They weren't spraying DDT."

Cully took a breath and jumped in. "What exactly was Dad doing before he left?" he asked.

Inca sat straight up as if pulled by an invisible thread.

"Well," she said, resting the book in her lap, "he was working on ideas for a new fuel, trying to find a method of running a car that doesn't use gas."

Cully nodded as he sat down on the little footstool beside the couch. "Dad said we would eventually run out of oil, and that gas is polluting the environment."

Inca smiled. "So you also remember Jack converted Lucky Lizzie's engine and her fuel tank, and then he spent hours experimenting with all sorts of things. You know, when your dad was a kid he always loved putting everything into a pot, making a mess. *Potions*, he called them. Well, he never did grow out of jumbling this and that together, and one day he said he'd come up with a potion that would work as fuel. It was fermented apple cider—what the old-timers call lumberjack hooch. Of course it was more complicated than just pouring a bunch of turned cider into the fuel tank. He had to cook it and tinker with it, and who knows what else—I'm telling you, he had the barn looking like a science lab."

"Yeah," said Cully, agreeing.

Inca tucked a wisp of copper hair out of her eyes "You know how we joke about how he's done everything—worked for the telephone company, been a security guard, a landscaper, a tree farmer, a truck driver. Even tried his hand at teaching."

"Opal says he's a Jack-of-no-trade because he never settles on anything," said Cully.

"I know," said Inca, making a face. "Opal can be hard on him. But I never saw Jack so excited about anything before. He spent hours working on this fuel—the Recipe, as he kept calling it. When Jim Bates opened his store, I know Jack started bringing some of our old things over there—pawning or selling this and that so he could buy equipment to make the recipe work better. Opal and Miggs would have been horrified if they had noticed, but Jack was careful about what he selected."

"So that's why he brought the watch in," said Cully thoughtfully.

"Watch?" Inca asked.

"Great-grandaddy's silver pocket watch," said Cully, immediately wishing he hadn't said anything.

Inca clapped a hand to her mouth. "Oh, that's terrible!" she exclaimed. "I remember now how serious and preoccupied Jack seemed at the time. I'll just march right down there and get that watch back—when—when I get the money for my book." She and Cully stared at each other, both miserable for a moment.

"But, Cully, there's more," she said, leaning forward and grasping one of his arms. "The night of your last birthday— remember? It was only a year ago, although it seems like several years ago." Letting go of Cully, she sat back and gazed dreamily out into space. "Opal made a perfect birthday pie for you, remember? The crust was as light as a summer cloud—I'm telling you, no one can make a pie like Opal."

"It was great," Cully agreed.

"After supper you and Jack went off fishing for a while."

Cully nodded, squeezing his arms tight around his knees, fending off a splinter of pain. He realized now how much he had been hoping his father would make it home for his birthday this year. "And then after we came back to the house, Dad went back to the truck and tinkered some more."

"That's right," said Inca. "He wanted to try out a batch of what he called the New and Improved Recipe. I don't really know what was improved about it—something about the percentage of—what was the word—*ethanol*—he was able to get out of it. And do you remember, he was reciting a poem at the top of his lungs the whole time he was pouring the new concoction into the fuel tank!"

Cully remembered. The moon had been full, the tree frogs were singing away, and Jack was reciting.

"I recollect it was 'Birches' by Robert Frost," said Inca. "Jack always said poetry would help Leapin' Lizzie run better!" She and Cully both laughed at the memory. "Well, then he climbed into the driver's seat, turned the key in the ignition, and the truck started right up. Remember how he shouted for us all to join him?"

Cully smiled. "Yeah, I sure do! And I remember how he ran and found an old mattress and threw it in the bed of the truck, and we all climbed in the back."

Inca nodded. "And he drove us all the way to the seacoast and back, the air smelling sweet from the exhaust of the apple fuel."

Cully loved that particular memory. The sisters had turned into girls, singing every song they knew in three-part harmony. When they got to the ocean they climbed out of the truck, took off their shoes, and ran around on the beach, playing tag with the moon-dazzled waves. He remembered his father throwing his arms around him and laughing and saying his success was all because of the poetry and the full moon.

"Well, the days went by, and Jack kept tinkering," Inca went on. "Then after a couple of months, he came to me and said, 'Incandescence'—he always calls me by my full name when he's excited—'I think I might have discovered something really important.'"

Cully leaned forward. "What? What was it?"

Inca shook her head. "He said it was top secret. He said he couldn't tell me just yet, but maybe he would in time."

"But he didn't tell you what it was?"

Inca shook her head again. "I never could follow all the ins and outs of it—too much chemistry—so I suppose he didn't bother trying to explain it to me."

"Oh," said Cully, feeling flat. He frowned and scuffed the floor with the edge of his sneaker. "Where is that Recipe, anyhow?" he asked after a moment.

"I don't know that, either," said Inca. "I know he was always scribbling things down on scraps of paper, but I have no idea where they are." She plumped a cushion on the peppermint-striped couch. "But honestly, Cully, there's something else that's bothering me." She paused a moment, biting her lip, looking as if she wasn't sure she ought to go on.

"What?" asked Cully. "Come on, you can say what it is."

Inca took a deep breath. "Your father signed up for the military, you know, right after he graduated from college."

"I know that," said Cully.

Inca picked up the cushion and held it in her lap. "But did you know his work in the military had to do with espionage? Spying?"

Cully's eyes grew big. "Dad was a *spy*?"

Inca looked around nervously, lowering her voice. "He didn't actually do any spying himself. I don't really know the particulars, but his work was more like the how-to part of things. How to blend in and not get noticed. That sort of thing. The point is, whatever he was involved in might explain why he suddenly bolted."

Cully leaped to his feet. "Do you really think so?"

Inca sat without speaking now, still clutching the cushion. The windows were open, and Cully could hear Miggs and Opal's voices drifting up from the porch.

"I don't really know," she said quietly, "but there isn't any other logical explanation for his disappearance. And— and I just hope he's all right."

Cully pulled out the postcard that was in his pocket and stared at it. "He *is* all right," he said firmly.

That night Cully had a dream.

In the dream Cully saw his shadow stand over him, take him by the hand, and pull him under the bed. Then he felt himself being squished and squashed and pressed against the floor. The sensation was weird but not painful, and after all the pressure stopped he was no longer under his bed or even in his room.

Cully was on a street where all the buildings, lampposts, trees, pavement, and sidewalks seemed to be made up of shadows. A bit of bright, flickering light caught his eye, and he gradually realized he was seeing his own body. His chest, trunk, and legs were illuminated, but he was as flat as if he had been run over by a steamroller in a cartoon.

Not only that, he was attached to some kind of... *personage*. He knew, in the way you do know about things in dreams, that the personage was actually his shadow, filled out and standing upright. He, Cully, was his shadow's shadow, only he wasn't dark the way a shadow is dark. A new word floated into his mind: he was a *lightow*—

Cully flowed along as his shadow walked, and he could see himself changing shape, bending up onto buildings, striping along fences or blades of grass, or becoming bumpy on uneven pavement. After a while he recognized the buildings. He and his shadow were in a shadowy version of the town of Medley. There was the bank, the office supply store, the jeweler, Pete's Parlor, the bookshop—and all the buildings were casting pools of light.

Another shadow personage walked by. This one didn't seem to have a lightow; in fact, as Cully looked around and watched other personages walk by, he saw several more without lightows.

Another shadowy personage approached Cully.

"Ih ereht, woh era uoy?" The other shadow seemed to be asking a question.

"Ton os doog," Cully's shadow answered, sounding very serious. Perhaps because as a lightow he was sort of a backward version of himself, Cully had no trouble at all understanding what was being said.

But as he listened he began to feel slightly angry, and the white light he was made of turned a shade of blue, rather like a white sweatshirt that has been thrown in the wash with blue jeans. His shadow said, "Eht wodahs-feiht sah neeb ta ti niaga," in a grim tone of voice. Cully felt a surge of real anger, and he turned a deeper blue.

"S'tel og gnihsif," his friend urged him. "I thguorb eht raeg."

"Lla thgir, doog aedi."

Both shadows began running; Cully flew along, sometimes behind, sometimes to one side, sometimes a little higher. They came to a place Cully knew by heart—the bank of the river where he and Sam liked to go fishing. As his personage cast a shadowy rod, the angry blue gave way to the color of pale moonlight. And then Cully realized there were two other figures on the bank, flanking him on either side. Their dark doggy forms were familiar and comforting.

In the morning, as Cully began to float up out of the dream, he thought about the name for what he had been—a lightow. He thought about his shadow, wondering if it could understand Cully when *he* talked, and whether it could feel anger or sadness. He recalled his shadow had said something upsetting: *Eht wodahs-feiht sah neeb ta ti niaga.*

Oh brother! He was thinking about everything as if it had really happened.

But the dream had seemed so *real*—Cully sat up in bed, frowning, the backward words *wodahs-feiht* turning themselves the right way around. *Shadow-thief.* Cully swallowed hard, thinking of Batty. He shook his head. It was only a dream, after all.

"Cully!" Miggs stuck her head into the bedroom. "Are you going to sleep all day?"

Cully heard the click of toenails on the wooden floor. Shep and Sheba pushed their way into the bedroom, nudging their noses into his covers, also demanding that he get up. Cully swung himself out of bed and put a hand on each of their necks. He was amazed and gratified that Shep and Sheba had followed him into his dream.

Cully and Miggs spent the morning scraping paint off the side of the farmhouse. The palms of Cully's hands were beginning to blister and his arms ached. "That's enough for today," said Miggs at noon.

After lunch Cully decided to go looking for the Recipe.

He started with Leapin' Lizzie. Although she sat out front in the driveway, Cully hadn't been near her in a while. Her front fender was dented, and the door on the passenger side was wired shut. He went around to the driver's side. This door opened just fine, and as he climbed in he was nearly bowled over with old-truck-just-sitting-there smell. It was mildewy and sour. Stuffing poked out of the seat, and there were definite signs of mouse activity. Dead yellow jackets lay in a heap on the dashboard. But Cully smelled a hint of something sweet, reminding him of one of Opal's apple pies.

Cully put his hands on the steering wheel. The key was in the ignition. He knew how to drive—Jack had let him drive around the property plenty of times. He put in the clutch and turned the key, but nothing happened.

He scooted over to the passenger side and pressed open the glove compartment. A sheaf of papers fell out along with work gloves, a spool of wire (probably for holding the door closed), receipts for work done on the truck, a box of Band-Aids, a pair of scissors, a book of poetry by Robert Frost, a plastic cowboy he had lost two years ago. Now that he had found the toy, he was too old to play with it.

Tucking Robert Frost under one arm, Cully jumped out

of the truck. He went into the house and all the way up the back stairs to Inca's Tower. Maybe he would find something up in the attic. Inca was bent over her worktable, Frank Sinatra crooning away, the sun streaming in through the windows.

"Going up to the attic," he called out.

He went into the little hallway between Inca's studio and the tiny room he slept in when he lived with Inca—it must have been a closet at one time—and with a pole and hook pulled down the attic door. The ladder came swinging down, and Cully climbed up.

A lot of things were stored in the attic—old clothes, for one thing. He found a sweater that had belonged to his mother. He buried his nose in it, breathing in just the slightest hint of sweet-smelling soap. And there was Jack's one suit, hanging up. In one of the pockets was an old drawing Cully had done of Shep and Sheba. He folded it up and put it in his own pocket. And then there, in the inside pocket of the suit jacket, was a sheaf of papers covered with his father's familiar scrawl.

Cully let out a whoop. "I found the Recipe!"

He brought the papers downstairs for Inca to see.

"Typical!" said Inca with a laugh. "He probably brought the Recipe to church with him and worked on it during the sermon. Okay, so let's see. 'Ten gallons of apple cider,'" she read out loud. "'Let cider sit outside for at least three days. Note: plain hooch'll cause the engine to stall, and probably rust the injector pump. Next: build yourself a tank with an internal heating element and cook the stuff.'"

Cully and Inca read on, finding more directions, diagrams full of arrows, and lists of parts to collect: liquid transfer pumps, an air pump, a 12-volt battery, a telescoping suction tube.

"I bet there's a lot of this stuff in the barn already," said Cully. "Think I can make the Recipe, Inca?"

"Well," said Inca cautiously, "it'll be a challenge."

5

Cully walked into Batty's Attic on Monday afternoon, and Isabel barged into the store a moment later, blowing on her acorn. Fitz's ears twitched with each high-pitched blast. It definitely wasn't Mozart.

Batty scowled at Isabel. "Is that noise really necessary?"

"Yes," said Isabel.

"What are you doing here at the store?" he asked.

"Isn't that a rude question?"

"Perhaps, but I really do want to know," said Batty.

"Your phone isn't working," said Isabel. "Kipper sent me here to tell you she's bringing another client this afternoon."

"Oh, sure enough, I left it off the hook again." As Batty replaced the receiver of his telephone, he scowled at Isabel. "Since when have you stopped calling your aunt *Aunt* Kipper?"

"Since the days you looked after me a whole lot more than she did," Isabel said flatly.

Batty rubbed the top of his head. "Don't you go trying to soften me up."

Isabel made a face. "As if I could. Cully, listen to how good I am." She put the acorn to her mouth and emitted another shrill whistle.

"Go take Fitz for his frisk," said Batty, putting his hands over his ears.

"Come on, we're going to perambulate, Fitz," said Isabel, picking up the leash.

Cully's heart sank. Once again he would be walking down Main Street with Isabel Ballou. Noticing the large shadow cast by Medley Savings Bank, he had a vivid recollection of his dream. Again he thought how real it all had seemed.

"You should see the dress I've been sewing," Isabel said as she trotted along beside Cully, holding Fitz's leash. "It's coming out so well. That's not bragging, you know. If you're good at something, it's okay to be proud of it. I'm the best memorizer at Medley Middle School. I won the Peebles Poetry Contest last year."

"I know," said Cully. He breathed a sigh of relief as they turned up a side street. The only thing worse than walking up Main Street with Isabel was the Peebles Poetry Contest. It was his least favorite assembly of the whole year. Kids droned on endlessly, some of them so softly you couldn't even hear a word they said.

Cully took Fitz off the leash and threw the ball, remembering how Isabel, in a frothy pink dress and ribbon in her hair, had gone on the longest. Only—he had to admit—she hadn't droned. She had been super-dramatic, marching around, waving her arms in the air, her voice getting louder and louder. It had been embarrassing. Lots of kids in the audience had begun to snicker. The teachers had frowned and said *shh.*

"Why are you looking at me like that?" Isabel asked. "Are you remembering the assembly and how kids laughed at me? I don't care because I won."

Fitz bounded up and dropped the ball at her feet. "I'm not

going to throw your muculent ball with your saliva all over it," she yelled at Fitz.

Cully picked up the ball and threw it again. He realized Isabel wasn't as oblivious as people thought. She had known kids were laughing at her but had gone on with her performance anyway. The aunts, who always came to Peebles because Inca had won the very first Peebles contest years ago, had been impressed. "For a girly-girl," Miggs had said later, "she's a gutsy little thing."

Spotting a blue jay feather, Cully thought maybe he'd give it to Isabel to make up for all the hard stuff in her life. As he bent down to pick it up, Isabel said, "What's that?"

"A blue jay feather."

"What's a blue jay?"

"You don't know what a blue jay is?"

"I bet I know a lot of things you don't know," said Isabel, nose in the air.

"I bet you do, too," said Cully, "like maybe you know what happens when your grandfather collects a person's shadow."

Isabel stopped walking and stood very still without saying a word.

"Have you ever gone back to his studio?"

"What if I have?" she asked.

Discouraged, Cully put the feather in his pocket and whistled for Fitz, who came right away. Connecting the dog to the leash, Cully strode off, not caring if he left Isabel behind.

Isabel ran to catch up with him. "He has a secret room, you know," she said, panting a bit. "Back in another hallway."

"What?" As they were coming out of the park a truck

rumbled by, making it impossible for Cully to hear. His heart sank as he saw a bunch of boys from his basketball team walking toward them.

"Hey, Pennyacre," said Nick Slater. He was carrying a basketball. "We're going over to the high school to play. Want to join us?"

"Maybe later," said Cully.

"Yeah, sure, get rid of the girlfriend, then you'll come," Will Suitor joked.

Cully felt himself turn completely red. As the boys loped off, Cully waited for an opening in the stream of cars and pulled Fitz roughly across the street.

"Hey, wait up," Isabel called after him. She caught up to him on the other side. "Did you hear what I said? About the secret room?"

They stood in front of Walker's Office Supply Store, staring at the stuffed animals holding onto pads of paper and pens in the window display.

"What about it?" Cully asked.

"The room has boxes in it," said Isabel. "Boxes and boxes."

"Okay. Boxes. That's nice."

"He keeps the room locked," said Isabel. "And I know where he keeps the key." She blinked slightly, and Cully was distracted for a moment by her long eyelashes. They reminded him of Inca's moths and butterflies, the way they were fluttering against her cheek.

"Key," he repeated.

"Yeah," she said.

"Have you ever been in there?"

"Once," she said. "I snuck in when Grandpa went across

the street to go to the post office. I was too scared to stay very long because I knew he'd get mad at me if he caught me snooping. I just poked my head in."

Fitz tugged on the leash. Cully started to walk again.

"I'm not really your girlfriend, you know," said Isabel.

Cully felt himself turn red again, this time with a sort of fury. As they approached the corner they saw Kipper's convertible parked at the curb. Mr. Masumoto, the nice, old Japanese man who ran the gardening center with his wife, was climbing out of it.

Mr. Masumoto's face lit up when he saw Cully. He had come to the farm a number of times to give Miggs lessons in Japanese farming. Cully often tagged along.

"I'm going to sell my vases," Mr. Masumoto said, nodding toward a carton he was carrying, "so Mrs. Masumoto and I can build a nice new home for our son. He is in Japan right now studying the old ways of gardening."

"You should do very well with your vases," said Kipper in a fluty voice. Her perfume wafted out behind her.

As Kipper marched with Mr. Masumoto into Batty's Attic, Isabel barged into the store, nearly knocking them both over.

"Isabel, where are your manners?" Batty scolded her. "And what are you doing here?"

"Your ballet class starts in fifteen minutes," said Kipper.

"I'm going, I'm going," said Isabel. She rushed over to the counter and, holding on with one hand, executed a few pliés. "I have to get warmed up first." She swept up an arm, and everything that had been on the counter went flying off onto the floor.

"Isabel!" Kipper and Batty both yelled at her.

"Oops, sorry," said Isabel. "Cully can pick up the stuff—I have to go."

"Thank you, Cully, that's a very kind offer," said Batty drily. He came out from behind the counter. "Now, good afternoon, Mr. Masumoto. I understand you have some special *objets d'art* to show me today."

As Kipper, Mr. Masumoto, and Batty sat down at the table, Cully bent down to pick up paper clips, pens, vintage postcards—even a coffee mug, which by some miracle hadn't broken. "I can't believe Isabel," he thought sourly, but as his fingers closed around a key, Isabel's strange clumsiness now made sense. He slipped the key into the pocket of his jeans, where it now sat next to the blue jay feather, his father's postcard, and his drawing of the two dogs.

Batty was busy looking at Mr. Masumoto's vases. They were pink and green and blue and gold, with birds and flowers on them. "These are exceptional, Mr. Masumoto," he said.

"Very beautiful," Mr. Masumoto agreed.

"I think you'll be pleased with my offer." Batty pushed back his chair and went over to the counter. He sat back down with a pad of paper and wrote down a figure and handed it to Mr. Masumoto.

Mr. Masumoto looked at the piece of paper. "This is enough to buy some land for my son and more," he said, tears coming into his eyes. "Thank you, Mr. Bates. I am so happy."

"O dear Mr. Masumoto, do please come back to my studio before you go," said Batty. "You see, I have a fascinating little hobby—I collect shadows, and I would be honored to add yours to my collection."

Mr. Masumoto's eyes grew large. "Shadow-collecting! Very unusual hobby!"

Shadow-thief. The words flashed into Cully's mind, and he felt horribly uneasy. He looked at Mr. Masumoto's trusting face, and then at Kipper, who had a too-sweet smile playing on her lipsticky lips as she sat there with the fat folder in her lap. APPLE BLOSSOM ACRES, the folder said in bold letters on the cover.

"Please give dear Mr. Masumoto a hand, Cully," said Batty.

Cully's heart began to race. "I'm not sure I can stay any longer today," he said nervously.

Batty stared at him for a moment and then smiled, exposing his broken tooth. "You're my apprentice, Cully, signed on for two weeks, at least. I need you. No need to run off just yet. We're ready to go to the back room now, dear Mr. Masumoto." He spoke too loudly, in the way people often speak to people whose native language isn't English. "You'll enjoy the process very much. It's an art form, like shadow puppets."

Mr. Masumoto clapped his hands. "This I love!"

Batty opened the door and let Mr. Masumoto through. Cully followed reluctantly, resolving to leave as soon as he was finished with the shadow-collecting.

As they came into the studio Batty said, "Now, dear Mr. Masumoto, please go and stand on that ample X. Cully, my excellent apprentice, is going to illuminate you. Such a nice shadow you'll make upon that wall."

"*Shadow* makes me think of puppets, but also of a famous proverb," said Mr. Masumoto. " 'The best fertilizer is the gardener's shadow.' This means gardener who tends and loves his garden provides the best nourishment of all."

Thinking how much Miggs would like that proverb, Cully turned on the light. Mr. Masumoto shivered slightly as his shadow sprang up on the wall. To Cully's dismay the shadow seemed thin and washed-out, more gray than black as Mr. Masumoto stood on one foot and twined his arms together, creating a long-necked bird with a long bill.

"I make crane," said Mr. Masumoto as the smell of chemicals filled the air. "My favorite bird."

"Now step away," said Batty.

Mr. Masumoto burst into gales of laughter as he saw his shadow being a crane without him. "Magic!" he exclaimed, clapping his hands.

Batty smiled. "No, no, my dear Mr. Masumoto, purely science. Now, Cully, assist Mr. Masumoto in his journey down the long, dark hall, won't you, and Mrs. Ballou will take him home."

Following Mr. Masumoto down the hall, Cully saw him pause a moment and then put a hand up to his heart. Cully rushed to his side.

"Are you all right, Mr. Masumoto?"

"I am old," said Mr. Masumoto.

"You're *not* old," Cully said, almost desperately. "You were just standing on one foot in there, and you're about to go and build a house for your son."

"Building is dangerous," said Mr. Masumoto.

"But—"

"I go back to my own little house now. It is safe there," said Mr. Masumoto, cutting Cully off.

Mr. Masumoto had changed, and so quickly—just like

Mr. Crimps. Cully stared at Mr. Masumoto's back as he shuffled along. Could it possibly be that Batty—but Cully couldn't see much in the poor lighting of the hallway. As he opened the door and they stepped out into the better-lit storefront, Cully's worst fear was confirmed. Everything in the room, including himself and Kipper Ballou, was casting a dusky smudge—everything, that is, except poor old Mr. Masumoto. Cully's heart began to pound uncomfortably.

Kipper was sitting at the table, the folder on her lap. "Rumor has it that you and your wife are thinking of building a new house for your son, Mr. Masumoto," she said with a smile. "I did want to tell you about some cute little cottages close by here. Save you the trouble."

"Yes?" Mr. Masumoto asked, perking up just the slightest bit.

"Apple Blossom Acres," said Kipper, opening her folder.

Batty came through the door to the storefront. He stood in the middle of the room, his eyes behind his glasses gleaming in an unpleasant way. "Everybody all set and happy now?" he asked.

Cully clenched his fists to make himself feel braver. "I—have to go now," he said. "And I'm sorry—I can't come back tomorrow. I—I can't be your apprentice."

Batty looked mildly surprised. "I'm honestly very sorry, too, Cully," he said, "because I have something of your father's you might want to know about. A rather important and valuable possession, in fact, and I'm not talking about that old pocket watch."

Cully stood rooted to the spot.

Batty patted down a few strands of hair. "I was, as it

happens, planning on taking the time to show you this possession tomorrow. As for today, a little sprucing up of the old place would be just the thing." Although Batty spoke lightly, Cully could feel the steeliness underneath his tone. "My, how dust settles on things. Makes them so drab, so gray—don't you agree?"

Kipper ushered Mr. Masumoto out the door, murmuring something about Apple Blossom Acres. Cully felt a mounting panic. His legs felt weak, and he could barely lift his arm to retrieve the duster Batty was holding out to him.

"Hey, Cully!"

Cully's afternoon with Batty was finally at an end. As he stood in a sort of daze by his bike on Main Street, he slowly became aware of the fact that Sam was shouting at him.

He felt a rush of relief when he saw Sam: good old sane and normal Sam!

"Let's go to your place and work on the highway," said Sam cheerfully.

Sam and Cully had been building a highway system for a set of small cars in the back of the barn for years. As the boys had grown older it had become more and more intricate and sophisticated, with ramps and tunnels and bridges. Cully thought working on it would be a good way to get his mind off Batty and his shadows.

Back at the farm the boys discussed the plans, brought out old boards, tried different things, but as much as he wanted to, Cully could not turn off his brain. After an hour of working, Cully kicked at a ramp and boards went flying.

"Whatcha doing?" Sam objected. "We had a cool thing going there,"

"We can build it again," said Cully, his pent-up feelings somewhat relieved for the moment. "Let's go fishing."

"Hey, fishing," said Sam enthusiastically. "You know what? I actually had a dream you and I went fishing the other night. It seemed so real."

"I had a dream like that," said Cully, looking at Sam in surprise.

Sam scratched his head and made a face. "Funny! Maybe we were both sleepwalking and we didn't know it."

Cully and Sam collected the fishing gear and then called for the dogs, who had been lounging outside the barn. As they raced happily ahead of the boys down to the river, Cully asked Sam, "Do you think shadows are real things?"

Sam's forehead creased into a wave of lines. "Real in what way?"

"I mean do you think they are a part of us, and if we lose our shadows for some reason it makes us different?"

Sam's forehead creased even more. "What are you talking about? If there's light, you have a shadow. No light, no shadow. A *person* doesn't change because of that." He spoke to Cully as if he were five years old.

"But what if there's light and you *don't* have a shadow?"

"Then you sprout wings and fly away," said Sam, twitching his line into the river.

Cully shut up. Sam was going to think he was crazy if he kept talking like this.

Cully cast his line into the river, too, and then sat down on the bank. Shep and Sheba sat, too, on either side of him, just like in the dream. It occurred to him that shadows were a bit like dogs, faithfully following you everywhere, sensing your moods. And like dogs, you had to pay attention to them.

Other concerns nagged at him, too, like how much did Isabel know about her grandfather's shadow-collecting hobby? Did she know what Kipper was up to with all those old people? He also wondered, not for the first time, exactly where Apple Blossom Acres was. He groaned inwardly, wishing he had never set foot in Batty's Attic. Building the highway in the barn and fishing were usually two activities guaranteed to bring him peace of mind. Nothing seemed to be working anymore.

"The black flies are wicked today," said Sam after a while. He swiped at the black bugs swarming around his head. "How about we stay here fifteen more minutes, and then if we don't catch anything we'll call it quits?"

The fifteen or so minutes passed without a fish nibbling, and Cully wasn't sorry when Sam said, "Okay, that's it. I'm not standing out here just to feed the bugs! Gotta get home, anyway. I'm learning to make cheese with my dad."

Cully felt a stab of envy, a new sensation for him. As he and Sam walked along the path back to the house, he mulled this over. If anything, he and Sam had a lot in common. They both lived on a farm. They both liked being active in the outdoors. They both had dads not tied down to office jobs. But now Sam had a father right there at home with him, and Cully didn't.

Sam was walking on the path just ahead of Cully. Before

he could stop himself, Cully blurted out, "My dad invented a new kind of fuel."

"Yeah?" Sam turned around to look at Cully with interest.

"And that's where he is right now, trying to sell the fuel all over the world." Cully felt foolish, like a little kid bragging about something he wasn't even sure was true. "He's going to make a fortune with it." Maybe, just maybe, some part of what he was saying was true.

"Wow, that's cool," said Sam.

"Ya want to hear about the fuel?"

"Yeah, natch I do."

As Cully reeled off the Recipe, Sam's eyes grew wider and wider.

"Found my dad's notes," Cully went on. "I'm going to try to make it. I bet you could help me. You're way better at science than I am."

Sam began whistling like a bird, which started the dogs barking. "Be fun to see a truck run on apples," he said finally, and then he reached out and punched Cully lightly on the arm. "I'm sorry your dad went off somewhere," he added quickly, before taking off at a run.

Cully felt himself blushing. Sam was having a hard time believing fuel could be made out of apples. He probably thought Cully was falling apart because his dad had gone off somewhere. And who could blame him? First Cully had kicked apart their construction, and then he'd asked weird questions about shadows, and just now he'd babbled on about apple fuel.

Cully knelt in the path, and Shep and Sheba came bounding over to him. He put an arm around each furry body and said, "But guess what? I'm not falling apart, because it's all true. Something does happen to you when you lose your shadow, and Dad did make a fuel out of apples, and that fuel works." Shep licked his face. "Yeah, Shep, and you know it's true, too, don't you?"

June 18, 1963

I just got a brilliant idea. I'll bring Grandaddy's moth collection to Batty's Attic. A lepidopterist once told me it was worth a fortune. If I can get some money for it, Opal will be less worried. I can also check in on Cully and make sure that Jim Bates is treating him well. Poor Cully didn't seem like his easygoing self tonight. After supper we were sitting on the porch and I asked him how his apprentice job was going, and he snapped and said, "I don't want to talk about it right now." He must be missing Jack like crazy.

6

"Good to see you, Cully, my boy," said Batty affably as Cully reluctantly came in the door. "I was a tad worried yesterday you might be giving up on me. Fitzy-Fitz here wouldn't like that," he added as the dog scrambled to his feet to greet Cully.

Cully was saved from having to say anything when Isabel burst thought the door.

"Did you get the key?" Isabel asked a moment later as they were walking down the street with Fitz. She was all in pink again: pink top, pink shorts, pink sandals with pink flowers poking up between rose-petal-pink toenails.

"Yeah," he said. He felt for the key in his pocket. It was there with the postcard and the blue jay feather and his childish drawing.

"I always figured Grandpa keeps his most valuable stuff in those boxes—chests of rubies and emeralds and diamonds."

Cully cast a sideways glance at Isabel. Her tone of voice was a little too casual. She knew something, he was almost sure of it.

As they entered the woods Isabel let Fitz off the leash, and the dog bounded off, nearly knocking over a group of girls who were walking up the path in their direction. They were all girls who managed to make life difficult for Cully at school.

"Hi, Cully," said Karen, smiling brightly. On Valentine's Day, she had stuffed his homeroom desk with thirty Valentines.

"Hi," said Cully flatly.

"Hi, Cully," said Mandy, also smiling brightly. All spring she had written Cully notes and left them in his cubby.

"Hi, Cully," said Tina, giggling. For a period of about two weeks, she had called Cully almost every night until Miggs told her not to.

All three girls completely ignored Isabel, and then as they moved on Mandy said, a little too loudly, "Can you believe Cully Pennyacre is hanging out with Isabel Ballou? What does he *see* in her?"

"Remember Peebles?" asked Tina.

The girls dissolved in a fit of giggling and pranced away.

Isabel's face turned red. All at once Cully was seized with fury. What was he doing with this stupid girl, anyway? Everything about being Batty's apprentice was putting him in a terrible position. He stood and faced Isabel squarely. "So do you know what your grandfather is really doing, or don't you?"

"Maybe I do, and maybe I don't," said Isabel lightly.

Cully whistled for Fitz, and when Fitz came running, Cully clipped the leash to his collar and began striding out of the woods. He had had enough.

"Wait up," Isabel called after him.

Cully walked faster.

Isabel ran to catch up with him. "You're mad at me. I

know why, too. 'Cause of those girls. You're embarrassed to be seen with me. Everyone's always mad at me or doesn't like me." Cully still didn't answer. "I know he actually takes people's shadows," she yelled after him.

Cully stopped dead in his tracks.

"Peaches and cream, what it takes to get you to slow you down," she complained as she ran up to him.

Cully frowned. "And what else do you know?"

Isabel stared at him for a moment, twirling a strand of hair around one finger. "I'll tell you if we go get something to eat. I had to get up at six to swim laps, and I never ate breakfast. I'll pay."

Cully was hungry himself. "Okay," he said, "but why do you *do* all those lessons?"

"It's how I pay back Kipper and Bobo for adopting me. I want them to be proud of me."

Cully jammed his hands into the pockets of his jeans. "Wouldn't they be proud of you anyhow?"

Isabel made a face. "You don't know Kipper and Bobo."

Cully tied Fitz to a bench outside Pete's Parlor. At the counter they ordered muffins, and then sat down opposite each other in a booth.

"Okay, spill the beans," he said.

Isabel took a breath. "One day, maybe two months ago, I came into the store crying after school because Mandy had a party where she invited every single girl in our class, every girl except for me. So I told Grandpa I wanted to have a party at the most expensive restaurant in town, and then we'd go roller-skating and to the movies, and I'd invite everyone, even the boys—everyone except for Mandy."

Embarrassed, Cully kept his eyes on his muffin.

"So Grandpa said, 'I've been a bit concerned about you lately, Isabel. I think I need to run a test on you.' We went back into his studio, which he hadn't let me into since we moved to this town. I don't know why—in every other store we ever owned, he always let me play in the back. Anyhow, he told me to go and stand on the X." She paused for a moment. "You know about the shadow-maker, right?"

"I guess so," said Cully.

"Well, Grandpa turned on the light and said, 'Just want to be sure.' 'Sure about what?' I asked, but he didn't answer—he just kept fiddling around with his chemicals. Even though I've seen my shadow up there when Grandpa turns off the light a million times, it always seems—I don't know—like magic."

"I know," said Cully, "but weren't you nervous? About losing your shadow?"

Isabel nibbled delicately at her muffin before she went on. "Why would I be nervous? I'm under twelve."

Cully frowned, not understanding.

"If you're under twelve, your shadow can't separate," Isabel said, as if she were explaining an easy math problem to him. "Shadows separate only if you're *over* twelve."

"I didn't know that," said Cully.

Isabel made a scoffing sound. "Well, anyway, Grandpa turned off the shadow-maker and slathered the chemicals on my shadow. He got out his tweezers and said, 'Now we'll just make sure.'" Isabel lowered her eyes. "My shadow peeled right off the wall," she said softly. "It never did before. I don't know why it did then." A tear slid out from beneath her eyelid and caught on one of her long lashes.

There was a thumping and a bumping as a group of laughing girls settled into the booth next to them.

"Guess what? Cully Pennyacre is here." Cully recognized Mandy's voice.

"He's sooo cute, and I'm just praying he's going to be in my homeroom again next year," said Karen.

"Shh, he'll hear you. He's sitting right there with guess who?" That was Tina.

"Is he still with Isabel Ballou? What does he *see* in her?" Karen asked, indignant.

"Maybe they're cousins and he *has* to spend time with her," said Mandy.

Isabel sat frozen, clutching her napkin. Then she unfroze and stood right up on the bench and peered over the back. "We're not cousins," she said.

The girls seemed stunned into silence. Mandy said, "Wow, Isabel, how do *you* get to hang out with Cully?"

"Why don't you ask *him*?" asked Isabel.

Cully slid down in his seat. He wanted to disappear under the table. The girls popped up and leaned over the back of Isabel's seat and started screaming. "Oh look—Cully Pennyacre! Everything we said is true—we *love* you, Cully Pennyacre." The girls, screeching and giggling, ran out of Pete's.

Isabel rolled her eyes. "Juvenile," she said.

Cully sighed. Being seen with one of the most unpopular girls in the history of Medley Middle School was proving to be a real trial.

"So about your shadow?" he asked when it was quiet again.

Isabel sighed. "I hate talking about this. Grandpa and I used to get along so much better. I told you how I spent a lot of time in all the shops he ever owned. He taught me neat stuff about old things, and he always liked hearing about what I was doing in school. He read really great books out loud to me and he taught me to use big words. He's the one who encouraged me to learn 'The Ballad of Sam McGee' for Peebles. He coached me and everything. Because we moved so much, I didn't make friends easily, but Grandpa was always there for me. But one day a few months ago he started being really grumpy and mean. I keep trying to think about what I did. I can't figure it out, except I guess I just have a bad personality. I annoy him like I annoy everyone else."

Cully tugged at his napkin, tearing it into little bits.

"Maybe he's being so mean because he's mad my shadow peeled off like that. I'll never forget the way he looked at me." Isabel shuddered. "He kept saying, 'My worst fear come true—a *loose* shadow!'"

The quaver in Isabel's voice made Cully look away again. "What did it feel like not to have a shadow?" he asked.

Isabel frowned. "It's hard to describe. I don't remember a lot about it. Just one thing—it was maybe a week before Peebles, and I'd been learning all those verses. I remember suddenly thinking, 'All the kids are going to laugh at me. What am I learning all this poetry for? So I can keep on being made fun of?'"

"But he gave it back to you," Cully said, noticing the faint smudges of shadow her hand cast in the not-very-well-lit booth.

Isabel nodded. "He walked over and washed my shadow in the sink. A second later I could tell my shadow came back to me 'cause I felt prickles everywhere, like after your foot goes to sleep."

"Hold on—" said Cully. He remembered Batty running Fitz's shadow under the faucet. "All you have to do to get a shadow back is wash it?"

Isabel shook her head. "That works only if you wash the shadow in the first fifteen minutes; otherwise you have to do something else—I don't know what."

Disappointed, Cully scooped the bits of shredded napkin into a pile. He had imagined somehow finding Mr. Crimps's and Mr. Masumoto's shadows and running them under water.

"I keep thinking if I'm nice to him, he'll forgive me for having a loose shadow," said Isabel. She started playing with the crumbs on her plate, looking forlorn.

"I don't think you have control over your own shadow," said Cully.

Isabel kept looking down at her plate. "That's not how he makes me feel. He makes me feel if only I were different—better—my shadow wouldn't be loose." She heaved a big sigh. "I'm surprised he didn't run a test on *you*."

"He did," said Cully slowly. "My shadow wouldn't separate. The weird thing is, I'm already twelve."

Isabel's eyebrows shot up. "You are so, so lucky!"

"But listen, the apprentice job—it's for kids between twelve and sixteen. So when I walked into the store to ask about the job, Batty right away said that thing he always says about his shadow-collecting hobby, and he took me back to the studio. He was so surprised when my shadow didn't separate—so don't you see? He was *expecting* my shadow to separate."

"'Course he was," said Isabel.

"No—the point is, he *meant* to take my shadow! I don't think he was looking for an apprentice at all."

Isabel stared at him, frowning. "Grandpa doesn't take kids' shadows. He told me that once. He takes only old people's, 'cause it doesn't hurt them that much."

"How does he know that?" Cully asked, beginning to feel angry.

"Old people are old, and—" Isabel didn't finish because Archie Sticks walked by their booth. He didn't see Cully and Isabel at first, but then he did a double take. "Whoa!" he exclaimed; then he smirked, raising his eyebrows knowingly. "Oh, say, sorry, didn't mean to butt in on the happy couple."

Cully sighed. Pretty soon everyone in Medley was going to think he was sweet on Isabel Ballou. As he scooted out of the booth, he looked at Archie, and an idea suddenly occurred to him. "Hey, Arch, come outside for a minute."

Archie was still hanging on the side of the booth. "What? You want to fight me?"

"No," said Cully. "I just want to get out of here. Fitz has been out there this whole time, and Batty is probably going batty because we're not back yet."

"You actually ended up working for that creep?" Archie asked as they headed out of Pete's. Cully saw, with a sinking heart, that Archie Sticks clearly did not have a shadow. Isabel trailed a few steps behind them. "My dad does some work for Jim Bates, and he says he's not a good guy. And by the way, Isabel, your dad isn't a good guy, either."

"Those are my *relatives* you're talking about," Isabel said indignantly. "And Bobo's not my dad, he's my uncle, and by the way, I wouldn't trust anything *your* dad says."

"Oh you wouldn't, would you?" Archie asked. "You think you're better than I am, but you aren't." He stalked off in the other direction.

"He is such a jerk," said Isabel, her face twisted into a scowl.

"There's a reason for it," said Cully in a tight voice. He felt as if he had just been kicked in the stomach. He'd bet anything Archie had lost his shadow the day he'd gone in to apply for the apprentice job. "He doesn't have a shadow."

Isabel stared at him, and he stared back. "You just made that up," she said. "You want to blame my grandfather for everything that's wrong with all the stuck-up people in this town."

"Believe what you want," said Cully curtly. He felt the way he had in the dream when anger had turned his body blue.

As they approached the store, Cully dreaded going back inside. It was only by some stroke of incredible luck that he hadn't lost his own shadow.

"So, you've been lollygagging about, have you?" Batty asked grumpily as they came into the store. A tall man in a three-piece suit was leaning against the counter holding a briefcase. "Mr. Colefax here and I have been waiting for you so we could go to the back room and conduct some business."

"Nice dog you have there," said the man, stepping forward to give Fitz a pat. He spoke with a pleasant English accent. To Isabel and Cully he put out a hand, saying, "How do you do? I—"

"Come on, Colefax," Batty interrupted, "we don't have all day. Now, where is that key?" he asked, rummaging through the clutter on the counter. Cully felt his heart leap into his throat, and Isabel became very pale.

73

Batty huffed slightly as he bent his round body down on one knee and started looking around on the floor. When he was sure both men weren't looking, Cully stealthily brought the key out of his pocket and dropped it into a glass jar filled with marbles. He waited one second and then said, "Is this it?"

Batty popped back up.

"There's a key in that jar," said Cully, trying to make his voice sound innocent.

Batty poked his nose into the jar. "Ah yes, good boy, you *are* a treasure." He plucked out the key and a marble along with it. "Here's your reward," said Batty, handing Cully the marble. It was an old cat's-eye, a marble with a slice of green in the middle. "It is worth something, dear boy. Very valuable, actually. Take good care of it."

Cully had always liked marbles—for one thing, he had been champion of the marble tournament in fourth grade. He tucked the marble into his pocket along with his other treasures.

"All right, my friend," said Batty, crooking a finger at Mr. Colefax, "come this way."

Batty walked across the store to a door where a long, dark coat was hanging on a hook; Cully had all along assumed it was a closet, but after Batty unlocked the door with the newly found key, he and the man disappeared down a hallway.

"That guy looks like a salesman," said Cully. "What do you think he's doing here?"

"Maybe he buys valuable antiques from Grandpa and sells them," said Isabel. She picked up the duster and started whisking around the room with it.

Cully looked at her closely. There was that tone in her voice again that made him think she knew more than she was letting on. Or maybe she was pretending not to know because she didn't want to.

The front door jangled open, and Cully was startled to see Inca come bustling in, carrying something bundled up in an old sheet. "Hello, nice dog," she said to Fitz, and Fitz's tail thumped vigorously in response. "Oh hi, Cully," she said.

"What are doing here?" he asked, eyeing the thing under the sheet.

"Selling some old doodads," Inca said lightly. "Maybe they'll bring in a little cash."

"What are you selling?" Cully asked, alarmed.

Before Inca could answer, they heard the sound of men's voices in the hall.

"Do not let Batty collect your shadow under any circumstances," Cully whispered fiercely in Inca's ear.

"What?" Inca asked, startled.

"I'm impressed, Bates, I really am," Mr. Colefax said, tapping the briefcase as he came back into the storefront. "You're one of the best suppliers around. I'll be able to turn this lot into a good product."

"Quality could be better in some cases—know what I mean, Colefax?" Batty asked.

Mr. Colefax raised his eyebrows at Batty. "No," he said shortly. "No, I don't. And I don't want to."

"Suit yourself," said Batty jauntily. "There are those who do."

"I'm sure I don't know what you mean." Mr. Colefax's manner was smooth, but he looked troubled. He set the briefcase on the counter and was about to open it. "Perhaps I ought to double-check the product you've supplied me with."

"I don't need someone half my age being hoity-toity with me," said Batty, flaring up. "And it's not a good idea to open your briefcase in here." He nodded significantly in the direction of Cully and Isabel and Inca. "Now then, Cully, apprentice mine, there is some old lumber out behind the store. I would like you to stack it to one side. Think you can handle that?"

"You were going to show me something—"

Batty's head jerked up. "Not a good time," he said curtly, "and I'd like to have that lumber stacked before you leave this afternoon."

Inca swept grandly over to Batty. "That is my *nephew* you're speaking to in that tone," she said.

Batty stared at her for a moment. "You mean to say you are another member of the great Pennyacre family? Well," he said, instantly becoming genial, "your nephew here is a great boon to me. Don't know what I'd do without him."

"I'm sure that's true," said Inca firmly. "He's a great help at home, too."

"Now then, Cully, my friend, I believe you have a job to do," said Batty. His tone was oily as he gestured politely toward the door.

Still wondering what Inca was doing at Batty's, Cully trudged unhappily out the door and headed around to the back. Isabel followed him.

"What's the matter?" Isabel asked.

"I hate what Batty is doing." Cully picked up one of the boards that lay scattered on the ground behind the store. He threw it angrily over to the side.

"That's my grandfather you're insulting," said Isabel,

turning red. "I don't go around saying mean things about your father, even though Kipper told me he ran off somewhere."

"Just go away," Cully shouted. He picked up another board and flung it as hard as he could.

"Okay, I will," said Isabel. She turned her back on Cully and marched away.

June 19, 1963

My world has just been tipped upside down. I went into town today and brought the Chest of Moths to Batty's Attic. I craftily concealed it under an old sheet, because I didn't want Miggs or Opal or Cully to start asking questions.

Well, first of all, Cully was at the store—silly me, I had forgotten he was working there—and he did start asking questions the very minute he saw me come in the door. He was with that girl who won the Peebles Poetry Contest, Isabel something. He also said a very strange thing about not letting Batty collect my shadow. And then Batty came in with this tall man who was wearing a nice-looking suit, and he started bossing Cully around. I don't think that old man is nice to Cully at all, and I must say he is funny-looking—a bit like a beach ball with glasses. And behind those glasses, his eyes look *fuzzy.*

I was thinking about all of this when I noticed that the tall man in the nice suit was staring at me.

O Diary, I must pause now to write this: Simon Colefax (I found out his name later), the man I am speaking of, has dark hair, lots of it, high cheekbones, violet eyes, a perfect nose, just the shadow of a blue-black beard, and a dimple on his strong chin. He looks like a model for a magazine commercial for men's cologne or fancy cars.

AND he has a divine English accent.

But I digress.

After Cully went outside to do a chore for Batty—and Isabel went out after him—Batty said, "And what can I do for you, Miss Pennyacre?"

When I told Batty why I was there, he rubbed his hands together and said, "Why, how unique! A Chest of Moths. Set it right down on that table and I'll take a look." As he pulled out each drawer, I found myself naming each moth—dear little Gray Half Spot and Bird's Wing and Green Marvel and on and on and on, and I knew suddenly that I couldn't part with the chest.

"I'm so sorry," I said, "I have changed my mind. I don't know what I was thinking."

"That's a shame," said Batty. "I don't recall ever having seen such a fine collection of moths—this collection should fetch you a pretty penny."

I admit I was once more tempted to sell the chest, but then I thought of Granddaddy and how much he had taught me—how to identify and catalog the moths, and how I should collect only a few of every species, not scads like so many collectors do. So I stayed firm and said, "I'm not going to sell."

Batty said he understood how important hobbies and collecting could be, and actually, would I indulge him in a harmless, innocent little hobby of his.

"And what might that be?" I asked.

"I collect shadows," he said.

An alarm went off in my head. That was exactly what Cully had told me I mustn't let Batty do. To cover up, I laughed blithely and said, "*Shadows?* How unique! How on earth do you collect shadows?"

And that's when Simon Colefax, who had been staring at me the whole time, suddenly asked if I knew how to sew. I said, "Why, of course I do," and he said, "I knew it! I had a feeling about you the moment you walked in here. Miss, er, Pennyacre, is it? I'd like to interview you for a possible job. Let's step out somewhere and discuss this, shall we?"

Batty looked surprised and quite annoyed as Simon swept up the Chest of Moths, saying he would help me carry it back to my car.

So there we were, walking down Main Street, me next to this perfect dreamboat. Honestly, I was so nervous I thought I wouldn't be able to think of a single thing to say, but I didn't have to think because Simon started asking me if I knew a lot about moths. I chattered away, telling him about Granddaddy and his collection, and then I told him I wrote and illustrated books about insects. He kept saying, "How interesting!" After we put the chest into the car, he said, "Now let's go somewhere for a cup of coffee and discuss what I have in mind for you." He even thought to put more money in the parking meter! Imagine being so thoughtful!

We went into Pete's, and the place seemed so dowdy compared to Simon. He is so elegant and cultured. But he looked around and said, "What a delicious place. So quaint!" We sat down, and he asked if I were in a position to take on some part-time employment. I ended up telling him how we are having a hard time making ends meet at the farm, and that it would be good for me to get another job. He told me that he, too, had grown up on a farm— can you believe it? He said he comes from Cornwall. Oh,

I was so envious. To come from Cornwall, England—how perfectly romantic! He travels all the time now for business, so he doesn't get home much.

But as we had strayed from the subject of the job, I said, "Mr. Colefax, just what is the work you had in mind?"

"Do call me Simon, please," he said. And then he said, "You're not going to believe it, Incandescence"—I had told him my full name, and I felt a little thrill as he said it—"but I believe this job was designed for you."

Well, I can tell you, dear Diary, that my heart skipped a beat as he leaned forward and—oops, I must stop. I hear someone coming up the stairs.

7

Cully stood in the driveway, trying to study Jack's diagrams for the Recipe. He was having trouble concentrating. Kipper Ballou had come by again last evening when they were sitting on the porch, saying she would offer the Pennyacres good money for some of their land. Miggs had actually stood up and shouted, "We're not interested!"

Kipper Ballou smiled her lipsticky smile and said, "So nice to see you again," and amid the frenzied barking of the dogs roared off in her convertible, once again leaving them on the porch in a gloom of too much perfume.

Cully glanced over at the dogs, who were lying in the shade of the barn. What, he wondered, did they sense in Kipper Ballou that sent their guardian instinct into action every time they saw her?

At least Inca had arrived home from Batty's with her shadow intact. And she was still carrying that thing bundled under the sheet, so she hadn't sold it, whatever it was. But she seemed even floatier than usual and impossible to talk to. And this morning, when Cully had asked her if she would help with the Recipe, she said she couldn't because she had to get ready to go out somewhere.

Cully frowned as he studied the Recipe—*what* was this word his father had written? *Transesterification.* Oh sure, he was supposed to know what *that* meant. And then what was this? *"1,000 ml of distilled water and one gram NaOH (lye). Be sure to wear long gloves, long sleeves, and long pants, and keep a big bag of kitty litter on hand to soak up the spills."*

Ugh. Why was it all so complicated?

Right then Sam showed up. "Whatcha up to?" he asked.

"Trying to make that apple fuel."

Sam stood and looked over Cully's shoulder at the diagrams. "Listen," he said after a while, "when you talked about apple fuel before, I thought the idea was a lot of hooey. But I see now your dad was applying real science. I'll try to help, if you like."

"For real?" Cully's heart leaped.

Sam grinned. "Got any cider?"

"There's a whole bunch that's gone bad in the back of the barn."

"Great! We're in business! We just need to find a large barrel."

The boys were about to pour jugs of fermented cider into a barrel they had set in the driveway when Isabel showed up. She wobbled up to them on a fancy bike a size too big for her. Her face was flushed. Shep and Sheba bounded up to her. "Get away, get away!" she screeched.

"They're just dogs, like Fitz," said Cully. "Um, Isabel, what are you doing here?" he asked, trying not to sound too mean.

"I got an idea," said Isabel. "About how we can find out more about the you-know-what."

"No," said Sam, frowning, "I don't know what."

"We can't say anything in front of him," Isabel said, eyeing Sam.

"You're the one who came here and brought the subject up in the first place," said Cully, immediately forgetting his resolve to be nice.

Isabel put her hands on her hips. "My grandfather is involved, and I don't want the whole world to know about it."

"Mr. Crimps and Mr. Masumoto and Archie Sticks are also involved," said Cully angrily.

Sam held up his hands. "Listen, if you two want to talk about this in private, I can leave."

"Good idea," said Isabel.

"No wonder your shadow won't stick with you," Cully muttered.

"What did you say?" she asked sharply.

"Nothing," he said. "Listen, Isabel, can we talk about this another time? We're kind of busy here."

Cully unscrewed the cap of a large jug of fermented cider and poured it into the barrel. The fumes from the alcohol stung his eyes. For the first time, Isabel seemed to focus on the barrel and the jugs. "What are you doing?"

"Something that I hope is going to make us rich so Ballou Real Estate won't buy my farm," said Cully firmly.

"What do you mean?" asked Isabel, her voice even raspier than usual.

"Your aunt is sniffing around our property."

"Are you *kidding*?" Sam sounded outraged.

Isabel hunched her shoulders. "I didn't know you were selling it."

"We're not," said Cully shortly.

Isabel looked as if she might cry. "Now I know why you don't like me."

"Oh, for Pete's sake," said Cully, exasperated. She twisted him up, making him mad one minute and sorry for her the next.

Isabel walked over to the barrel and peered into it. "What's this for?" she asked.

Cully shook his head in disbelief. "You must be crazy if you think I'm going to tell you."

"Okay," said Isabel, turning away. "I came here for nothing."

Isabel started to climb back onto the bike, but it fell over on top of her. The dogs rushed over, trying to help. "Peaches and cream," she said, lying there. "I told Kipper just to get me an old secondhand bike, but she had to go out and buy this thing." Cully hauled both Isabel and the bike up. Brushing herself off, she said, "Good riddance to bad rubbish," and climbing back on the too-large bike, managed to stay upright and pedal away.

"So you going to tell me what's going on, or not?" asked Sam.

As Cully took a breath, a black Cadillac purred up the driveway and came to a stop.

"Whoa," Sam whistled, "get a load of that gorgeous hunk of metal!"

Mr. Colefax unfolded himself from the car. Inca floated out of the house and onto the porch. She was wearing a gauzy, yellow dress and looked like a butterfly.

"Hello, boys," she said as she fluttered past them. "I'm off to work."

Mr. Colefax strode toward her. "Incandescence," he said, "what a vision thou art." He sounded even more British than he had the day before.

"Hello, Simon," said Inca, blushing, "this is my nephew, Cully, and his friend Sam. This is Simon Colefax."

"I believe I saw you yesterday at Batty's Attic," said Simon, beaming down at Cully.

Miggs appeared from around the corner of the house in overalls and a straw hat. "What's going on?" she asked, waving the pitchfork she was carrying.

"I'm off to *work*," said Inca proudly. "I'm going to be a seamstress!" She began walking toward the Cadillac.

"Hey, that truck's a beaut!" Mr. Colefax exclaimed suddenly as he spotted Leapin' Lizzie. Just as suddenly, he didn't sound British at all. "How much you sellin' her for?"

"How much will you give for her?" asked Miggs.

"Not selling," Cully said quickly.

"Three grand," said Mr. Colefax.

Miggs's eyebrows shot up.

"The truck belongs to my dad, and he's not here right now," Cully shouted.

"That's right," said Miggs after a moment.

Cully heaved a sigh of relief.

"Well, she's a beaut, all right—I mean, she is simply smashing," Mr. Colefax said, his accent crisping up again, "so if you have a change of heart, do let me know. Well, then," he added, "lovely to meet all of you, but we're off." He cupped a hand under Inca's elbow and led her to the car. Inca slid into the front seat as he held the door open.

In a moment the car purred off down the driveway.

"Uh-oh," said Miggs. She plunged the tines of the fork into the ground and rested on the handle. "Inca's been hooked again."

"Yeah, I'll say," said Sam.

"Who is he?" Miggs asked.

"He's a—I don't know," said Cully. "He was at Batty's yesterday and Inca met him there."

Miggs frowned. "What was Inca doing at Batty's Attic?"

"I'm—I'm not sure," said Cully.

"Well, I hope she wasn't trying to pawn anything for easy money. And what exactly is Inca going to be sewing?"

"I don't know," said Cully anxiously.

"Did I imagine it," Opal asked as she came out of the house and down the porch stairs, "or did I just see Inca go off with a man in a Cadillac?"

"You didn't imagine it," said Miggs. "Inca's been hooked again. And no doubt he's just as feckless as the others."

"Not this time," said Opal cheerfully. "She told me all about it. She got a job! She's sewing some sort of specialty item—cloaks, I think she said—for some important agency. Isn't it wonderful she found something so quickly?"

Miggs took off her hat and fanned her face, looking somewhat relieved. "Well, the job does sounds right up her alley; she is a beautiful seamstress. Just as long as she doesn't get too behind on *Mothology*."

But as soon as Miggs and Opal went back to what they had been doing, Sam said, "Say, Cully, you know what was weird about that guy, Colefax? He talked different when he was looking at the truck. He didn't sound so highfalutin. I don't think he really is English."

"Yeah," said Cully thoughtfully. "All I can say is, Inca really picks 'em."

"So let's get back to the Recipe."

Cully shook his head sadly. "Can't right now. I have to go to that apprentice job."

"You don't sound too happy about it."

"It's—say, Sam, want to come into town and help me? Just for a while?"

Sam shrugged. "Well, okay, I guess. I'm kind of curious about what you do there."

"Just one thing—if Jim Bates says he wants to collect your shadow, don't let him."

"Huh?"

"It's this weird hobby he has—just say no if he asks."

Sam stared at him oddly.

"That's all I can tell you for now, but promise me you won't, okay?"

Sam frowned. "Listen, Cully, are you sure you're okay? I mean, I figure you must be worried about your dad, and—"

"You don't have to come," said Cully, flaring up.

"Yeah, but I want to," said Sam lightly.

Sam climbed onto his bike, and Cully couldn't help laughing as he watched him pedal. Sam's legs were too long for his bike, and he looked like a clown in a circus act.

As Cully and Sam came through the door of Batty's Attic, Fitz greeted them with a thumping tail.

"Ah, you've brought a friend, terrific," said Batty, his face lighting up when he saw them. "I have some chores for you, apprentice mine, and your big, strapping friend can help."

"But you said you'd show me—" Cully started to say.

"Ah, all in good time, dear boy," said Batty, cutting him off. "It's not something—uh—to be shared with the general population. But don't worry, I'm keeping it on hold, just for you, as long as you are cooperative, dear boy. " He waggled his eyebrows at Cully, and Cully felt his stomach churn.

Batty set the boys to unpacking several large, tall cartons that were standing in the back of the room. "Make a list of everything you pull out," he said. "I'll be right behind the counter if you need anything." Batty left them alone, and Cully relaxed somewhat. As he and Sam pulled out old plates and glasses and dishes, he almost felt as if he had a normal job.

They had worked for almost an hour when Kipper Ballou burst into the shop. Following closely behind was Mrs. Towsley, the elderly owner of the magazine and newspaper and candy store in town. She was carrying a small box.

"Yoo-hoo, Pops!" Kipper called out. "I've brought a customer! Come on over to the table here, Mrs. Towsley, and have a seat. Batty will be right with you."

Batty came out from behind the counter. "Well, well, Mrs. Towsley. What have you brought me?" he asked.

"My little musicians," said Mrs. Towsley. She was a small woman. Her beady eyes darted all over the store, taking everything in. She reminded Cully of a friendly crow. "My little German grandmother collected them and passed them on to me." She put the box down on the table and, reaching in carefully, began unwrapping tissue paper. One by one she set up ceramic figures of children in lederhosen and skirts and kerchiefs playing musical instruments.

Batty picked up one of the figures. "These are in excellent shape," he said admiringly. He went over to the counter and picked up a catalog. "I believe they are turn-of-the-century and worth a great deal, Mrs. Towsley. I can look them up for you."

Batty handled the figures, consulted the catalog, and then scribbled something down on a piece of paper. Kipper sat in another chair, humming softly to herself. Cully watched with his heart in his mouth. Here was the setup all over again.

Batty finally handed Mrs. Towsley the piece of paper.

"My," said Mrs. Towsley, with little bird-like bobs of her head, "I can't believe it! I had no idea they were worth this much."

"I can give you cash for them, Mrs. Towsley," said Batty, jumping up from the table.

Mrs. Towsley wagged a finger at him. "Oh dear me, no, that won't be necessary, Mr. Bates, I just brought them in here to find out how much I should insure them for. I'm planning on passing 'em down to my grandson, the way my grandmother passed 'em down to me."

"Are you sure, Mrs. Towsley?" Kipper looked flustered. "Think of what you could do with a little extra money."

"Thank you so much for the information," said Mrs. Towsley. She began to wrap up the figures again. "I'll just be going now."

"Before you do," Batty said hurriedly, "you might, er, humor me for a moment. I have a little hobby—shadow-collecting—"

Sam's head snapped up out of a box; he stared at Batty curiously.

"Oh, really?" Mrs. Towsley put down the figure she had been wrapping. "What kind of hobby is that?"

"Please, dear Mrs. Towsley, come back with me to my studio and I'll show you," said Batty politely.

"Well, I don't mind if I do. Sounds intriguing," said Mrs. Towsley.

"Oh, and Cully's friend, you come, too," said Batty. "I am willing to wager you have never seen anything like this."

Sam took a step toward the middle of the room. "I *would* like to see that—" He stopped suddenly, glancing at Cully. "Actually, maybe not right now, Mr. Bates. I gotta be going in a minute. Gonna just finish up the last of this box." As his head disappeared back into the carton, Cully breathed a sigh of relief.

Batty raised his eyebrows. "Just need to remind you, Cully: I do expect you to be discreet about certain aspects of my business, and there is no need, by the way, to come back into the studio today."

Cully watched helplessly as Mrs. Towsley followed Batty. She walked with quick, little steps and a strong, straight back. He dreaded seeing how she would walk when she came back out.

"I'll just go and run some errands while Pops is in there," said Kipper, getting to her feet. "Nice to see you, Cully—do give my best to your lovely aunts—and oh, you are Sam Cleary, aren't you?" she asked, taking a step toward Sam. "Your family owns that huge dairy farm on the other side of town." She reached into her purse and brought out a card. "I hear dairy farming is not so profitable these days. Have your parents give me a call. Maybe we could work out something."

Sam laughed. "I don't think so," he said, turning away.

"Much better to think positive," said Kipper, pressing the card on him, and Sam took it in spite of himself. The door jangled noisily as Kipper went out.

Sam ripped up the card and flung the pieces on the floor. "She's like a beached whale!" he exploded. Then, startled, he flung up his arm. "Ow! Something just pinched me."

"Naw, she's more like a sick cow—ow! Something just

pinched me, too," said Cully, frowning. He rubbed the back of his arm. "There must be some kind of gnat in here."

"A sick cow's too good for her—sick cows are to be pitied—ow!" Sam yelped again and bent down, rubbing his shin. "Something just *kicked* me. What the heck is going on?"

Fitz was up on his feet now, tail wagging as he pressed against the air as if something were there to press against. Puzzled, Cully reached out, and his fingers closed around something soft and silky that he couldn't see. He yanked, and Isabel's face, flushed with suppressed merriment, appeared, floating in midair a foot away from him.

"Jiminy," Sam cried out. "What the—"

Isabel's hands appeared, and then her entire body.

"I found a cloak made of shadows," Isabel said, almost squealing in her excitement. "It's been hanging all this time right there." She pointed to the door that had the long, black coat hanging on it. "And it—makes you invisible!"

"Jumping Jehoshaphat," said Cully, seeing how the cloak blended with the other shadows in the room. He reached out to feel the soft silkiness again.

Sam couldn't keep his fingers off the cloak, either.

"It's what I was going to show you when I came over," Isabel said to Cully. "But then you were mean."

"I wasn't mean, I was—"

They heard the sound of Batty's voice behind the door and saw the doorknob turning. Isabel threw the cloak over her head and disappeared.

Mrs. Towsley, followed by Batty, came through the door looking stoop-shouldered. She walked around the counter and over to the table with a shambling gait. She was no longer bird-like at all. Jerking a thumb toward the ceramic children, she said, "You take those, Mr. Bates. Got to thinking my young grandson's not the type to appreciate 'em anyhow. Young people don't appreciate anything these days. Just take 'em off my hands, please."

"Ceramic figures of this type are fetching a pretty price right now," said Batty.

"Oh fiddlesticks," Mrs. Towlsey growled. "Stop yammering and take 'em."

Shaking slightly, Cully walked over to the table and picked up one of the figures. He deliberately began wrapping it in tissue paper. Whatever Batty had of his father's couldn't be worth as much as a person's shadow. He couldn't stand by watching people being tricked by Batty anymore.

"Just what are you doing?" Batty demanded.

"Putting these things away," said Cully. Sam watched Cully, his mouth hanging slightly open.

Batty strode angrily over to Cully and was reaching for him when Isabel popped out from beneath the table. She stood in front of her grandfather with her hands on her hips.

Batty whirled around, staring at her. "What? When did you sneak in here?"

"I've been here all along," said Isabel tartly. "You just didn't notice me, like always."

Mrs. Towsley had been standing in the middle of the room, a dull look in her eyes, not appearing to follow what was going on, but when she saw Isabel her face brightened. "Now, there's a lass after my own heart. I bet *you'd* appreciate these, my dear."

Isabel looked startled. "Me?"

Mrs. Towsley came over to the table, swept up the figures, and thrust the box into Isabel's hands.

"I—I can't take these, Mrs. Towsley," Isabel stammered.

"Nonsense, my dear, you look just like my little sister who died of the whooping cough. She loved this little collection, and it makes me happy to think about you having it." Mrs. Towsley's shoulders sagged another inch. "And you don't want an old woman to be unhappy, do you?"

"There you are, Mrs. Towsley, how are we doing?" Kipper asked, bustling in the door.

"I don't feel so good," said Mrs. Towsley. She ran a hand over her face. "Don't know what's come over me. Gotta get home now."

Kipper was holding her folder. "Now, Mrs. Towsley, I was thinking about you the other day—living all alone in that apartment above the store. You must be getting ready to think about retiring. There's going to be a pretty little community right near here called Apple Blossom Acres. Everything will be taken care of for you and—"

"Don't have the funds to retire," Mrs. Towsley cut her off grumpily.

"A little down payment," Kipper said smoothly. "I'm sure your set of figurines—"

"Didn't sell 'em. Little girl has 'em."

Isabel, clutching the box, had been watching, her face growing paler by the moment.

"Isabel?" Kipper looked flustered.

"Take Mrs. Towsley home, Kipper," said Batty. "We'll talk later."

As soon as Kipper and Mrs. Towsley were gone, Batty

marched over to Isabel. "All right, missy, you can put that box down now."

Isabel narrowed her eyes at him. "Mrs. Towsley gave her collection to me," she said.

"She didn't know what she was doing," said Batty.

"She didn't know what she was doing when she brought her stuff to you in the first place," Isabel retorted.

Sam looked from Batty to Isabel to Cully. "I'm getting out of here," he said. "I need some fresh air."

"Me too," said Cully.

"Me three," said Isabel.

Cully and Isabel followed Sam outside. Sam turned on Cully. "What the heck is going on in there?"

Cully walked quickly, trying to get his nerves to settle down. "Come on, let's go to the woods. I don't want to talk here."

Isabel trailed along behind, carrying Mrs. Towsley's box. Once in the woods, she stopped beside a hollowed-out stump. "I know Kipper will go through all my stuff looking for these, so I'm going to hide them in here."

Cully tossed a stick into the river and watched it twist and turn in the current. The swirling water matched his feelings.

Isabel suddenly started appearing and disappearing. "Now you see me, now you don't," she giggled. Then she explained, "I had to ditch the cloak in a hurry, so I stuffed it into my pocket."

Sam shook his head. "What kind of gimmick is this exactly?"

"I don't mind anymore if we tell Sam everything," Isabel said shyly.

Sam crossed his arms in front of his chest. "About time, don't you think?" he asked.

"You wouldn't have believed us earlier," said Cully.

"Might not believe you now," said Sam, "but shoot."

They settled on a tree trunk that had fallen across the river. Taking off his sneakers, Cully let his feet dangle in the water. Sam did the same, but Isabel's legs were too short. She perched awkwardly, as if she had never sat on a tree trunk before in her life.

"So," Cully began, "if you saw with your own eyes that Isabel can become invisible, you can believe what I'm going to tell you now about Batty and his shadows."

Cully launched into the whole story. Sam listened, not moving a muscle.

At the end he whistled. "Jim—i—ny."

"And you heard Batty invite you back into the studio. He was going to take your shadow," said Cully.

"You don't know that for sure," said Isabel, but she hunched her shoulders unhappily.

No one spoke. They heard the sounds of traffic on Main Street and the *tut tut tut* of a nuthatch. A man walked by with a beagle, and then, to Cully's dismay, he saw the Girls: Karen, Mandy, and Tina. As the Girls got closer, they started squealing. "Cully Pennyacre! Sam Cleary!" They acted as if Isabel were invisible, and Cully, checking, saw that she was. He tapped the air beside him and made contact with her elbow.

"We're going to the movies, wanna come?" Karen asked.

"No," said both boys at the same time.

"Oh, you probably want to hang out with *Isabel*," said Mandy.

"And learn *poetry* for the Peebles contest," Tina cackled.

The girls screeched with laughter and then moved on.

Cully reached over and pulled the cloak off Isabel. She sat with her arms wrapped tightly around her bent knees. She reminded Cully of one of those insects you prod and they curl into themselves.

"Don't pay any attention to them," said Sam kindly. "They're idiots. They could never win the Peebles Poetry Contest."

Isabel wiped her tears with the back of her arm.

Sam leaped off the tree trunk. "Listen, Cully, probably everything you just told me is true, but I've had enough for one day."

Cully jumped off, too. As they came out of the woods, he stared at the shadows the three of them cast on the sidewalk. Elongated in the afternoon sun, they looked as if they were walking on stilts, with small knobs for heads.

"Wonder if my shadow can be separated," said Sam. He started leaping and waving to himself.

"Don't even think about it," said Cully, his hands forming fists.

"Hey," said Isabel, stopping suddenly and pointing across the street, "there's Mr. Colefax."

"And Inca," said Cully. Inca and Simon Colefax were walking together, laughing. "Let's follow them," he said suddenly. "Where's the cloak?"

Sam groaned. "I'm outta here. I gotta go home and milk the cows." He ran a hand across his face. "Cows. Now there's something I can understand."

Cully hated to see Sam leave—he felt so much braver with him there—but before he had time to think more about it, he felt the soft silkiness of the shadow cloak brush against his face. Darkness lapped around him and then quickly gave way to a grainy shadiness. As he looked around, everything appeared to be in black and white as if he were viewing an old movie.

"Come on," said Isabel impatiently. "Let's cross the street. They're heading for that big, black car."

Simon was handing Inca into the passenger side of the Cadillac. Cully and Isabel reached the car just as he went around to the other side. Cully was thankful the Cadillac had four doors—most cars didn't. He and Isabel were able to dive into the back just as Simon turned the key in the ignition. The car shot out of the parking space and raced up Main Street.

Inca gasped, "Simon, that's a red light—"

"Love that color red!" said Simon with a chuckle.

They shot by the last gas station in town and surged up the "Footpath," the name given to the road that had once been followed by Indians on foot. Now it was heavily traveled by trucks, cars, and motorcycles.

As the road twisted and turned, Cully felt himself growing carsick, and from his vantage point in the backseat Inca seemed more fluttery and nervous than usual. She kept patting her hair and turning her head to glance at Simon.

"Just where exactly are we going?"

"To the job," said Simon.

"Oh," said Inca. "I was wondering when we would get to that. It has been a lovely day, really, going for a picnic and walking by the river, telling stories and laughing—but I did wonder when I'd start working."

Simon was following a slow truck up the hill. He

suddenly gunned the engine and lurched past the truck as a motorcycle came roaring toward them. Isabel was thrown against Cully. She dug her fingernails into his arm. Inca clutched the handle above the window and screamed.

"All right, Bozo, keep outta my way," Simon shouted. He leaned on his horn as the Cadillac swung back onto the right side of the road just in time. "That was some fun, huh?" he asked, laughing.

"Wasn't that a no-passing zone?" Inca asked faintly.

"You're not getting on my case, are you, lady?" Simon asked her playfully.

"I was just wondering," said Inca. She was quiet for a moment, and then, clearing her throat nervously she said, "And another thing—I thought you were English, but maybe I was mistaken?"

"Of course I'm English," said Simon, immediately tightening up his accent. "Can't imagine why you'd think otherwise, my dear. And here we are." He spun the wheel to the right, and the car swung into a parking lot.

Gazing out at the black-and-white world, Cully saw they were at the Lookout, the observation tower on the Footpath. It was perched about halfway up the hill and boasted extraordinary views, although as a tourist attraction the place always seemed to have trouble making a go of it. Now there was a sign that said **FOR SALE**.

In spite of the wooziness from the ride, Cully was able to open the door and stagger out of the car. He and Isabel stood together under the cloak in the parking lot.

"Here we go, my lady," said Simon, going around to hand Inca out of the front seat.

"Ooh, I used to love this place," said Inca cheerfully as

she looked around. "I remember when they had a petting zoo and an ice cream stand. Just what are we doing here?"

Simon, meanwhile, opened the trunk and took out a basket. "Come with me, and you shall see." He took Inca's hand and led her over to the bottom of the stairs, a rickety-looking set that wound up and up.

A large sign saying NO ENTRY, KEEP OUT, DANGER was attached to a heavy chain hanging across the entrance to the stairs. Simon swung one long leg over.

Inca hesitated. "It says No—".

"You *are* a stickler for rules, aren't you?" he said, lifting up the chain for her. "Come along, don't dillydally."

Cully and Isabel hurriedly scooted under the chain after Inca, not easy to do in tandem while trying to keep themselves covered by the cloak. They followed Mr. Colefax and Inca up stair after stair. The guardrails looked flimsy.

"Oh my word, Inca, you look magnificent in this light," said Mr. Colefax suddenly.

Cully, peeking out from under the cloak, thought Inca did look beautiful set against the sky. She reminded him of a red-headed Fay Wray in *King Kong*, which he had just seen on the *Million Dollar Movie Show*. The sun was setting; lights were already twinkling in the valley. A steady stream of headlights ran along the main roads of Medley. But Cully was brought back to reality as the wind came up and the whole rickety structure creaked and swayed. He felt Isabel's fingernails digging into his arm again.

"Are we going any higher?" asked Inca in a quavery voice.

"This is it," said Simon. "We are now standing at the best place in the county to gather moths." He pointed up at a yellow light dangling from a wire. A cloud of moths flittered and fluttered around it. "Here it is, the porch-light parade. Your task, my beauty, is to point out the Sleepy Underwing. I myself wouldn't know a sleepy one from a wide-awake one, so I'm counting on you."

Inca peered up at the moths. "There's a Lace-Border and a Brindled Sphinx, but most of the moths appear to be Sleepy Underwings."

"I was told this is the best place in the county for Sleepies," said Simon. "So now then, to gather their shadows."

"Shadows?" Inca asked uncertainly.

"I'll demonstrate." Simon pulled a spray can out of the basket and, aiming the nozzle at the moths, pressed. There was a *psssh* sound, and the moths quivered for a moment in the air. Their shadows detached and fell into the basket he was holding. The moths themselves ceased to flutter, and soon spiraled limply down through the air.

"That's how it's done," Simon said with satisfaction.

Inca stood on the landing, shivering and biting her lip. "You're killing the moths when you do that," she said.

"They're *moths*," said Simon.

"I know they're moths," said Inca. "You just don't go around killing batches of them, except for the coddling moth, which goes after apples."

"Let me explain something to you," Simon said without a trace of English accent. "The thread you're going to use to sew the cloaks is made from moth shadows. For some reason the shadows of Sleepy Underwings make the strongest thread."

Inca plucked the can out of Simon's hand and flung it over the edge.

"What are you doing?"

"I'm not going to kill moths, and I'm not going to stand here and watch you do it, either."

Simon exploded. "No, you're not, because you're fired." He turned and stormed down the stairs at such a mad clip that Cully and Isabel had barely enough time to squeeze out of the way.

The tower creaked and shook as Simon made his way down. At the bottom he flung himself over the chain, and a moment later the Cadillac leaped to life and roared off down the hill.

Except for the yellow light and the battering of moths around it, darkness and silence settled on the tower.

8

"Hello, moths," said Inca softly. "You're safe now, but I better think about getting down from here and getting home." She sighed slightly. "It will be a long walk."

Cully and Isabel followed Inca as quietly as they could. At the bottom Cully steered Isabel over to a shabby ticket booth and stepped behind it. "I'm going to let her know we're here," he whispered, throwing off the cloak.

Hoping he wouldn't startle Inca too much, Cully stepped out from behind the booth and called out gently. "Inca! It's me, Cully!"

Inca put a hand to her heart. "Cully! What a surprise! What are you doing here?"

"Isabel and I were—looking for—for moths," said Cully. "What are *you* doing here?"

"Why, Isabel Ballou, here you are again," said Inca, peering at Isabel in the fading light. "But oh, Cully, I've gone and made such a fool out of myself. *Again.* And all because of a man. *Again.* You'd think I'd have learned a thing or two by now. That Simon Colefax wanted me to collect moth shadows, and they can't survive, poor little moths, without their shadows. But now that I know about this spot, I'll have to come back here. I saw the most beautiful Cecropia. Oh, I don't know why I fell for that Simon Colefax—he seemed such a charming English gentleman—but obviously he's no gentleman—"

"Or English," said Isabel.

Inca looked angry. "How could he drive off like that and leave me to walk down the Footpath in the dark? It's not even safe to walk down it in the daylight!"

They heard the sound of a car coming up the hill. Headlights beamed into the parking lot as Simon's Cadillac swung off the Footpath.

Cully, who had been holding the cloak, flung it over the three of them. He was glad Inca was only an inch or so taller than he was. They all just managed to be covered. "We're invisible now," he whispered, "so don't say anything."

"I've always wanted to be invisible!" Inca exclaimed.

"Shh," Cully hissed, nudging Inca with his elbow.

There was the sound of a car door opening, a crunch of gravel underfoot. "Incandescence? Inca, where are you?"

Simon strode about the driveway, swinging a flashlight, investigating one dilapidated structure after another. He shone the flashlight up the stairs. "Inca! For Pete's sake, where the heck are you?"

"He's *not* English," Inca whispered.

A pickup truck suddenly rattled into the parking lot. The lights turned off, the doors opened, and a man got out and began walking unsteadily across the lot.

"Colefax? Is that you?" a man asked in a thin, high voice.

"Yes," said Simon, straightening up. "You're late." He spoke in his English accent, in control of himself again.

"Had some trouble with my boy," the man said. "He got in a fight with some other boys, and I couldn't get away.

He's—he's not himself. Used to be such a good boy." Cully suddenly realized the man was Dwayne Sticks, Archie's father. What was he doing here?

Now a sporty, red convertible swept into the parking lot. Isabel squealed, clutching Cully's arm, and Cully bit his lip as he recognized the Ballous' car. A tall man climbed out and walked toward them.

"What the—" Dwayne exclaimed, his voice tinged with fear.

"Robert Ballou," said Bobo Ballou, striding over to Simon. "Jim Bates told me I would find you here."

"I don't believe we've met," said Simon cautiously.

"I work for SPY," said Bobo, handing Simon a card.

"SPY," repeated Simon. He sounded surprised. "That's one of the top three organizations."

"As you can see, I'm very well-connected," said Bobo.

"Since when are *you* in this business?" Dwayne demanded. Cully thought Dwayne was trying to sound tougher than he felt. "I thought *your* job was to bully people like me who have trouble making their payments. Just so you know, this is *my* turf."

"Doesn't have your name on it, as far as I can see," said Bobo lightly.

Isabel was squirming, and Cully had to keep a firm hold on her to prevent her from throwing off the cloak.

"Let's see your product, Colefax," said Bobo.

"This is not your turf," said Dwayne again, a desperate edge to his voice.

Simon went over to his car and opened the trunk. He brought out a box and carried it over to the two men. Bobo squatted down, going through the contents with a small flashlight that cast a strange, purple light. "Looks like fine work," he said.

"Fine enough," said Simon with a sigh. "It's not easy to find good fabricators."

"Got anything in the twelve-to-sixteen age bracket?" asked Bobo.

"Of course not," said Simon sharply. "That's where I draw the line."

Bobo laughed pleasantly. "Of course," he said, "but we all know the young 'uns make for darker, denser cloaks."

"You—you!" Dwayne spat. He whirled in a fury on Bobo, grabbing the taller man's collar with both hands. "You ever say that in front of me again," he shouted, "and I'll—I'll—"

"Get your dirty hands off me!" Bobo snarled, wrenching himself free.

"If you don't mind, I need to get going," Simon said, stepping between the two men. Speaking in a voice he clearly was trying to keep steady, he added, "I've got ten adult cloaks with me. One thousand dollars apiece. You can take 'em or leave 'em."

"I'll double that amount and take them all," said Bobo calmly. Dwayne groaned but did nothing as Bobo reached into his jacket and withdrew a wad of bills. "Charmed to do business with you, sir," he said, handing the money to Simon. "Until the next time."

Bobo picked up the box and sauntered, whistling, toward his car. A moment later the sports car roared off down the hill. Simon stayed right where he was, counting the money. Dwayne didn't move, either.

"Er, sorry about that, Sticks," said Simon, sounding

apologetic. "Listen, stay in touch, I'll see what I can do. Maybe I could get some more cloaks made up—"

"You don't understand," said Dwayne, his voice thin and tight. "Jim Bates told me he'll hold onto my boy's shadow as long as I give him a cut on every cloak I sell. If I don't come through, he'll—"

"He has your *boy*'s shadow?" Simon's voice rose with shock, and Cully felt Isabel grip his hand.

"Psshh," said Dwayne, shaking his head. "You don't even know the half of it. You don't even..." His voice subsided into an incoherent mumble as he stumbled off, and then a few moments later Cully pulled Isabel and Inca well out of the way as Dwayne's truck rattled out to the edge of the parking lot and then clattered down the hill.

"Oh you stupid doofus, Colefax!" Simon shouted into the silence that followed. "How did you manage to get mixed up with this horrible business?" He headed for the Cadillac.

Cully prodded the others. "Come on," he whispered. "We'll get a ride."

"I don't want to ride with him," Inca whispered back. "He *is* a stupid doofus."

"They're all stupid doofuses," said Isabel, not bothering to whisper.

Cully understood why they wouldn't want to get back in the car with Simon Colefax. The meeting they had just witnessed had shaken him up. Here was poor Dwayne Sticks trying to hold onto his son's shadow, and Bobo Ballou, Isabel's uncle, was involved in some way, throwing large sums of money around. Cully shuddered. Bobo seemed like a mean man. Cully turned to look at Isabel. She wasn't even bothering to cover herself up with the cloak anymore, and she looked miserable.

But the idea of walking down the Footpath at night with drivers like Dwayne Sticks on it was not appealing.

"Come on," Cully said, pulling Inca and Isabel across the lot. "Get back under the cloak, Isabel."

Simon was already climbing into the Cadillac by the time they reached it. The three of them managed to pile into the backseat just as he started the car.

"Drat that female," Simon muttered. He gunned the engine, and the Cadillac shot out onto the Footpath, narrowly missing an oncoming car. The passengers in the backseat clutched each other as Simon sped up and barreled down the hill.

"Slow down," Inca gasped.

Simon's head spun around. "Huh? Who's there?" Not seeing anyone, he spun his head back.

" 'Tis the ghosts of moths," Inca intoned, drawing out the words in a wail. "You think moths don't matter, but they do. And slow down!"

Simon swerved dangerously. He pulled over onto the not-very-wide shoulder. Several cars whizzed by. "This business has finally gotten to you, old buddy," he said out loud. "Better quit before you lose your mind."

"You already have," Inca moaned.

Simon was no dummy, and after all, he knew about spy-cloaks. Sure enough, he reached back with one arm and whipped off the cloak.

9

Simon turned on the interior light and swiveled around to stare at the three stowaways. Isabel cowered, covering her head with her arms. Cully slumped as far down as he could get. Only Inca remained upright, as calm and dignified as if she were sitting in church.

"There are three of you!" Simon exclaimed.

"Yes," said Inca in her ghostly voice.

"Knock it off!" Simon shouted.

"What's the matter with you, Simon?" Inca asked in an ordinary voice.

"Give me that cloak. You stole it from me."

"I don't steal," said Inca indignantly.

"One of these kids, then," he said in disgust.

"Tell me about your farm in England," said Inca.

Simon pounded a fist against the seat, but he didn't answer. Cully was madly calculating—should they try to escape? He inched his hand toward the handle, but Simon noticed. He reached back and pressed down the lock button. "Oh no, you don't," he said. "Don't imagine I'm going to let you go that easily."

Simon swung up his hand and turned out the light and started the car. He roared off the shoulder, and there was silence as the Cadillac sped down the hill.

Inca leaned forward and put a hand on Simon's shoulder. "Listen, Simon. We're almost at the bottom of the Footpath. Just pull into that car dealer's, will you? I want to talk to you."

Simon hunched his shoulders, still not speaking. As they reached the bottom of the hill, he pulled into a lot filled with cars and turned off the engine. They sat beneath a large sign saying **Footpath Cars** in glowing, blue letters.

"You said you wanted to talk, so talk," said Simon sulkily.

Inca climbed out of the car and went around to the front and slid in next to him. "Don't be so angry, Simon," she said. "You're the one who left me up on that old, rickety tower, remember? I don't understand why you turned on me like that. And I thought—I thought—you *liked* me for *me*." Inca sounded close to tears. "I didn't realize you were using me for my sewing skills and my knowledge of moths."

Simon turned to Inca. "Look, I'm under a lot of pressure. I have to produce a certain number of cloaks, or I'll be beat out by the competition."

"And I'm under the impression this is not a *legal* business," said Inca primly. "Otherwise you would not be meeting people in out-of-the-way parking lots in the dark of night."

"Legal or not, secret agents need spy-cloaks," said Simon grumpily.

"You seem much too nice to be in this shadow business," said Inca in a disappointed tone of voice. "How did you get involved in it?"

Simon shook his head. "I used to be a car salesman. Cars, that's what I know—cars and their engines, like this baby," he said, patting the dashboard. "Then I heard about a job opening for an international salesman in spy-cloaks. Seemed like a step up. I took a training course. Learned who the shadow-collectors are, how to pick out good fabricators. Learned how to speak like an English gent so I could sound classy and sell cloaks to spy agencies all over the world. They even gave me Midnight Molly here to drive." He patted the dashboard again. "That's what I call her—Midnight Molly."

In the neon blue light, Inca's face looked severe. "They're a bunch of thugs, Simon, bribing you."

"We would never win wars without these cloaks," Simon said, staring straight ahead.

"Haven't you thought about where the shadows come from?"

Simon sighed, hunching his shoulders.

"Simon? We're talking about real people here. You heard Dwayne. Something has happened to Archie."

"I just *make* the cloaks, you know. I prefer not to know about that other stuff." A weighty silence followed. Simon nervously drummed his fingers on the dashboard. Then he turned to Inca and said, "To tell the truth, I don't really fancy the cloak-making part of the job. I can never find a reliable fabricator. The product's got to be quality—can't have a cloak falling apart on you in the middle of an assignment—very embarrassing. That's why I was so excited when I met you and—"

"Simon, this is a bad, bad business."

Simon hunched his shoulders up past his ears and stopped talking.

"I'm *not* making cloaks for you, Simon."

Simon drummed his fingers some more. "It doesn't

matter," he finally burst out. "It doesn't matter because I'm quitting."

"You're *what*?"

"I'm quitting!" Simon was bouncing on his seat. "I'm done with shades and shadows, cloaks and daggers. I don't know how I'm going to make a living now, and I'll miss Molly, here, but I need a good dose of decent folks—like you, Inca, I mean. Before I worked in this business, I never would have deserted a lovely lady on a dangerous tower—"

"I hope you wouldn't have deserted *anyone*," said Inca, sitting up straighter.

"Aw, you know what I mean."

Inca didn't say anything for a moment, and then she said, "Simon, I think you are a gentleman after all, even if you're not from Cornwall."

"I *am* from Cornwall—Indiana—beautiful farming country—wish I'd never left it."

"Well, then, you'll like our farm," said Inca. "Come and stay with us until you get your feet back on the ground."

"I don't want to be mooching off you—"

"Oh no, you wouldn't be mooching," said Inca. She was leaning toward Simon now, full of enthusiasm. "We've got a cute little house no one's living in at the moment—we call it the Chicken Coop, although it's not a chicken coop at all—and you can pay us rent. We sorely need the extra cash. And we'll put you to work—I know my sister Miggs could use an extra hand."

Cully could hardly believe his ears. Inca was installing *Simon Colefax* in the Chicken Coop? "Who's going to feed him, Inca? *You*?" he demanded. During his four months with Inca, Cully had learned what a terrible cook she was.

"He'll just have to get used to a lot of macaroni," Inca said defensively.

"I can cook," said Simon gruffly.

"And you can drive us home now, Simon, nice and legally and under the speed limit. I do like following rules, and besides, there is no point in getting stopped by the police."

Simon started the car, and as they began to cruise toward town he turned on the radio. "Wise...men...say...only fools...rush...in," sang Elvis Presley, "but I...can't... help...falling in love...with...you."

FROM INCA'S DIARY:

June 22

All this awful shadow stuff! I am so glad Simon isn't involved with it anymore, and he is being such a big help around here. Each day he sheds a little more of the English gentleman and becomes more down-to-earth. He is pitching in with the house painting and is very good at the difficult parts around the windows. He pulled away the rotten parts of the porch and is starting to rebuild it. He dismantled the cider press and oiled the parts.

You know what is a really strange coincidence? I am remembering now that whenever we asked Jack what he did when he was in the army, he always said he was working with shadows! Of course he said it with that grin of his, and at the time I thought he was just kidding around, not wanting to say what he really did. I thought perhaps "shadows" was a code name for something else.

Simon told me when you lose your shadow, your whole personality becomes extreme—poof—just like that. All your quirks, all your bad qualities become exaggerated. I hate to think what I would be like if I lost my shadow!

This makes me think about how moths start off as eggs and then they turn into caterpillars and then pupae and then winged creatures. Insect metamorphosis is as amazing as any story told in Greek mythology. But in real life it's not an instant transformation; it's a slow process. Imagine forcing a caterpillar to turn instantly into a moth or a butterfly. People and caterpillars should never be forced to change.

10

"This is my last day," said Cully as he came back from his walk with Fitz at the end of the week. Isabel had not come by the store, not even once, and Cully wondered if after the Mrs. Towsley episode she had been ordered to stay away, or if she was staying away on her own accord. And Batty still had not shown Cully a single thing belonging to his father.

"Your last day!" Batty exclaimed. "Ha! Let's not make a precipitous departure, my boy. On Monday I will close up the shop so that no one will interrupt us, and at that time the item I have in my possession that belongs to your father shall be revealed."

Cully sighed. He would come back once more, on Monday, but not one more day.

On Sunday afternoon Simon popped up Leapin' Lizzie's hood and was astonished to discover the converted engine.

"What is this?" he asked Cully, who was standing nearby.

Cully hesitated only a moment before telling him about the Recipe.

"Fantastic," Simon exclaimed. "I'd like to try it."

Cully shook his head. "We don't have any more of the fuel, and it's very complicated to make. My dad, he's the one who came up with it, but—he's not here—and you know about my dad, right?"

Simon nodded sympathetically. "Your aunt did tell me a little about him. I'm real sorry he's not here. But hey, Cully, there's no reason why you and I shouldn't try to get that fuel to work. Pretty nifty if we could!"

Cully shook his head again. "I've been trying, but I'm having trouble with it."

"Let me take a look," said Simon, and Cully reluctantly went into the barn and pulled the Recipe out of a box he was keeping it in. Simon studied the diagrams for a time. "I think," he said finally, "I have the gist of the Recipe. Let's get this baby rolling!"

They worked all afternoon putting together tubes and gaskets, and Cully finally felt comfortable enough to ask the question that had been on the tip of his tongue for days. "Mr. Colefax—" he started to say.

"Know what, kiddo?" Simon interrupted, "I don't go for this mister stuff. I'd like you to call me Scooter. That's the name my friends call me."

"Okay, Scooter," Cully said, instantly feeling more at ease. "Is there really a big difference between young and old shadows? Like what Mr. Ballou was talking about?"

"I'm not sure what you mean," said Scooter.

"That night at the Lookout when Mr. Ballou was buying cloaks from you, he talked about how young shadows are darker and denser," said Cully.

"Oh geez, that's right. I forgot you were there." Scooter ran a hand across his face, leaving a smudge of grease on his nose. He sighed deeply. "Yes, there really is. It isn't that noticeable until a shadow is stripped—I mean, the average person probably wouldn't be able to tell, but an expert can spot an older person's shadow right away. So generally speaking, you get more money for the juveniles. Mind you, shadows in general aren't that easy to come by. Shadow-stripping isn't exactly legal anymore, although in times of war, hot or cold, business picks up. Spies in every country benefit from being invisible."

"So people get tricked into giving up their shadows," said Cully angrily.

Scooter hunched his shoulders. "Years ago, the spy agencies used the shadows of criminals. Or of prisoners of war. Not a good thing, I grant you, but—"

"Batty has been taking the shadows of ordinary, innocent people who live around here."

Groaning, Scooter ran a hand across his face. "The truth is, I never met a shadow-collector who wasn't a little—well—shady."

"And not just old people's—he took my friend Archie's shadow."

"Yes, I know," said Scooter, looking miserable. "And for kids, losing their shadows does a real number on them. Makes them very unstable."

"Isn't there anything we can do?" Cully asked.

Scooter frowned. "If I'd known about Archie earlier, I'd have gotten his shadow out of Batty's stockroom, but I can't go back there now. Batty is furious at me for quitting. And the truth is, even if I had Archie's shadow in my hands right now, I wouldn't know how to reattach it." Simon picked up a piece of rubber hose. "But what do you say we leave off talking about all this for a while, Cully, and get back to more wholesome topics, like making apple fuel?"

That evening Cully found Opal and Miggs sitting together at Miggs's kitchen table with papers spread out before them. "What are you doing?" he asked, alarmed. Opal rarely sat in Miggs's kitchen.

"Figuring out a way to keep going," Miggs said, looking tired. "If we put off fixing the roof, and we don't buy a new tractor..."

Cully retreated to his room. He picked up the book of poems by Robert Frost that was on his bedside table. The book fell open to "Birches." He sat on the bed and started to read.

> When I see birches swing from left to right
> I like to think some boy's been swinging from them,
> But swinging doesn't bend them down to stay, ice storms do that.
> Often you must have seen them on a sunny winter's morning.

"Yeah, I *have*," said Cully out loud. The voice of the poem sounded as if Jack were speaking to him.

Cully put the book aside and stared out the window. The light of the waxing moon filled the room. Jack's baseball trophies made a design of bumpy shadows on the wall. "Scooter and I are gonna make that fuel, Dad," he said softly.

From Miggs's diary

I see I haven't written anything in ages.

Ma always encouraged us to keep a diary—she thought it would be good for us to get into the habit of recording our thoughts. Truth is, I've come to find recording what seeds I've sown in the garden more interesting than my own thoughts—but today, for a change, I just have to write.

I finished the weeding this morning and made sure the pea vines are growing up straight on their supports. And then I headed over toward the birch tree that stands at the base of the hill—I have been keeping my eye on this Luna moth cocoon—it's on one of the lower branches of the birch tree—and, well, I just happened to be in the right spot at the right time. I heard this rough, ragged sound, and what do you know, Luna was tearing herself out of her silk casing right at that moment—and then there she was, out in the sunlight, with her lovely light green wings and antennae that look like feathers. I wish Inca had been there to see the whole thing.

But anyway I was actually feeling plenty good about life, in spite of the dark cloud of debt that's always hanging over the farm. When I'm outside working, tilling the earth, feeling the sun on my back, watching moths emerge from their dark houses, I am almost certain we will find a solution to our troubles.

I decided to go up the hill to the boulders and talk to

Ma, and I wasn't even winded when I got to the top, even if I am an inch past thirty-eight.

Shep and Sheba loped up the hill with me, and I was thinking how mighty glad I am we still have those two dogs. So many people they've seen come and go over the years—Ma and Pa, and Tabitha, and Melvin—and Jack, of course. If they could speak, I bet they would be asking, Where the heck is that Jack?

Up at the top of the hill, I could see down to Route 5 and the river and the railroad track. I could also see the orchard and Simon Colefax fixing the wire mesh we put up around the trunks of the trees to protect them from deer and mice. Scooter, as I guess we're calling him now, is turning out to be all right—way better than I expected one of Inca's men to be.

I could also look down at the house and the garden and the bare maple tree. I always think of Jack when I look at that tree—him playing in it when he was a boy, creating that little Mouse House in its roots to hide his treasure box.

Is Inca right? Is that tree grieving for Jack?

"Where the heck are you, Jack?" I asked out loud.

Then the dogs and I sat down by Ma and Pa's boulder. "You'd be pleased with the garden this year, Mom," I said. "There will be lots of green and wax beans, and the rhubarb has already come in good."

Then I turned to look at our woods behind me on the hill. I got to thinking maybe we could bring in some cash by logging some of the trees. And that's when Shep and Sheba started running around in circles, barking like crazy.

"What's gotten into you?" I asked, but then Sheba started growling in a way I recognized, and sure enough I heard that woman's voice not so far away in the woods behind me. "Hush, dogs," I said. "We have to be very quiet and find out what she's doing here."

I pulled Shep and Sheba behind the big pine tree and made them sit, and then, peering out, I could see Kipper Ballou and two men toiling up the path that winds up the other side of the hill. I kept my hands firmly on Shep and Sheba's necks, and they were pretty quiet, except for a rumble and a grumble here and there. Those three intruders were huffing and puffing by the time they made it to the top. It didn't help that Kipper was wearing a ridiculous pair of tottery shoes, and the two men were lugging surveying tools.

"So am I right, or what?" Kipper asked. "Isn't this the best view in the county?"

"Don't see what difference a view is going to make for what you're doing," one of the men complained.

"Now then," said Kipper, all serious and businesslike, "we're looking at building one-story storage units, from 40 to 80,000 square feet of rentable space—we'll want direct drive-up access and enough outside parking for boats and motor vehicles. We'll build cheap and get big dollar returns. On 40 acres, how many of those units do you reckon I can build?"

Storage units? Kipper Ballou wanted our land for storage units?

Well, I let go of the dogs on the spot, and Shep and Sheba ran at them like mad bulls let out of a pen, barking and yapping and snarling. I thought Kipper and those men were going to pass out on the spot. Then I stepped out from behind the tree and said in a very civilized tone of voice, "You are trespassing, and if you don't get off my land immediately, I shall have you arrested." One of the survey men said, "I thought you had permission," and then the two men picked up their gear and hightailed it down the hill.

"You're losing a big opportunity here," Kipper said, and then she turned tail, too, as Shep and Sheba chased her all the way down the hill.

Well, one thing I know—that's the last we'll see of her!

11

"All right, my friend," Batty said to Cully on Monday. "The shop is locked; time for revelations. Come this way."

Batty led Cully through the door that had the long, dark coat hanging on it, down a hall, and into a room filled with boxes and boxes stacked up on floor-to-ceiling shelves.

"Now then," said Batty. "Our subject matter would be invisible to the human eye without these special, fluorescent lights." He flicked a switch on the wall, and the room was washed with an eerie, purple light, reminding Cully of Bobo's flashlight that night in the parking lot. Batty slowly ambled down a narrow aisle between shelves, poking here and there at a box. "We're looking for P—Pennyacre." He stopped suddenly, slapping a hand to his forehead. "But of course—the Pennyacre folder is on the Pending shelf."

Cully thought Batty knew exactly where the folder was and that he was just adding drama to the moment; sure enough, now Batty headed straight for the far end of the room, and after perusing the shelves for a moment, all the while hemming and hawing—more drama—he pulled a box toward him and removed the lid. He reached in and brought out a manila envelope.

Cully shivered as he saw *PENNYACRE, JOHN I.* written across the envelope in black block letters. Batty bent up the metal clasp, opened the flap, and withdrew a dark shape, which he then shook out as if he were airing a suit of long underwear.

"There we are," said Batty.

"Is it—is that—"

"Your father's shadow? Yes."

Trembling slightly, Cully stretched out a hand. As his fingers made contact with the soft, silky substance, a vivid and distinct picture of his father sprang into his mind—it was almost as if Jack, tall and lanky, with his straight, reddish-blond hair falling into his lively, brown eyes, were standing in front of him.

Cully lunged for the shadow, but Batty quickly yanked it out of his reach.

"Tsk-tsk," Batty said. "Let's not be grabby."

"It doesn't belong to you," said Cully angrily. His entire body was beginning to shake.

"It does," said Batty calmly.

"You shouldn't be taking people's shadows from them!" Cully shouted.

"Purely voluntary, my friend," said Batty, not at all fazed by Cully's anger. "You've seen how eager people are to have me collect their shadows."

Cully swallowed hard. "Saying you collect shadows as a hobby is not telling people what you're really doing."

Batty shrugged. "A failure of imagination on their part."

"They sell their old stuff to you—"

"And I *pay* them for it," Batty cut in, sounding offended.

"Yeah, and then they hand all that money over for—for—for—Apple Blossom—whatever it is."

"Once again, it's all purely voluntary, dear boy," said Batty, his voice light and unconcerned.

"Everything you do is rotten," Cully cried. Furious, he kicked the box that had contained the shadow.

"Careful," Batty said, frowning now, the light tone gone. "I'd like to point out that your father's shadow is on the Pending shelf."

"What does that mean?"

"About to be processed," said Batty, waving the shadow in the air.

"*Processed?* You mean turned into a spy-cloak?" Cully began to feel panic swirl through him.

Batty pulled on his lower lip, looking annoyed. "I don't know how you know about spy-cloaks—perhaps that Colefax fellow has been flapping his trap, and he'll be sorry if he has—but I'll tell you this, Cully: separation stirs up the molecules, so I usually wait about six months for things to settle. It has been just about that amount of time since I obtained Jack's shadow, and honestly, I could fetch a nice price for a healthy, dark piece of goods like this one." Batty folded the shadow over one arm and gazed affectionately at it. "But, Cully, my friend, just to demonstrate how much I value your assistance, I've decided to keep your father's shadow as long as you stay and work for me. Isn't that nice of me? And really, dear boy, you mustn't keep raising a fuss every time Kipper brings a client into the store. That scene with Mrs. Towsley the other day was thoroughly unpleasant."

"You can't have *my* shadow, so what else do you want from me?" Cully asked angrily.

"Ah, Cully, I've only just begun to explore your usefulness—a popular, clever boy like you. But we mustn't spend any more time back here. People will be wondering why the store isn't open today." Batty folded up Jack's shadow—arms first, then legs, and then the head tucked neatly down. He slipped it into the envelope and then back into the cardboard box. "Nighty-night," he said, giving the lid a gentle tap. He walked the box over to a shelf marked HOLD.

Batty motioned for Cully to go out first, then he turned off the purple lights and shut the door tightly and locked it. "Just so you know, Cully," he said, "I keep this useful little item right here." He smiled, holding the key in front of Cully's nose, and then dropped it into his breast pocket. "Wouldn't want it to vanish and then mysteriously reappear in my jar of marbles, eh?"

Batty smiled genially, and Cully remembered Inca telling him that sometimes collectors killed moths by putting them in a bottle with the lid on tight. That was how he felt now—as if he were imprisoned in a bottle with no air to breathe, no way to escape.

As they came out to the storefront, Batty went over to the front door and unlocked it. "So," he said, rounding on Cully severely, "I expect you to keep your opinions to yourself if Kipper brings someone in here."

Cully didn't answer.

"But my, my, it is awful dusty around here," Batty went on, changing his tone. "O apprentice of mine, I'd dearly like it if you would dust all the shelves."

Cully had to struggle to make himself stay in the store, but he took the duster from Batty. As he began to dust he was distracted by a movement just to one side, a little behind him. He turned and stared. His shadow was pointing. At first he thought he was imagining it, but then he looked again and sure enough, his shadow was using the duster as a sort of baton and pointing it in the direction of the door where the long, black coat was hanging.

Cully scratched his head, but instead of scratching with him the shadow stuck out its shadowy arm and pointed again. In spite of the shock of having a shadow that was acting as if it had a mind of its own, Cully put one foot in front of the other and walked toward the door.

It slowly dawned on Cully what his shadow wanted him to do. He cast his eyes around the shop, thinking quickly. "I keep seeing this weird-looking cow thing on that shelf over in the corner," he said to Batty. "What is it, exactly?"

Batty's back was turned long enough for Cully to reach out and grasp the spy-cloak that was hanging against the long, black coat. He stood on tiptoes, freeing it from the hook.

"Is this what you're speaking of?" Batty picked up a white porcelain cow just as Cully stuffed the cloak into his pocket. "You lift the cow's tail, and the cream pours through the mouth. Milk straight from the cow! Big collector's item."

Cully knew perfectly well what a cow creamer was— there were dozens of them on a shelf in Opal's kitchen. The door jangled open, and Fitz lifted his head and wagged his tail as the store was suddenly filled with Karen, Mandy, and Tina.

"I told you he was working here," said Mandy. "Hi, Cully."

The Girls swarmed all over the store, sifting through boxes of buttons, trying on old hats and costume jewelry. Karen grabbed the creamer from Batty, exclaiming over it.

"Girls, girls," said Batty, flapping his hands at them.

"Oops, sorry, Mr. Bates, we should be more careful with your stuff," said Karen.

"No, no," said Batty, trying to smile. "It's a pleasure to have young people in the store for a change. Listen, girls, I have a harmless little hobby—I was wondering"— but he was interrupted by Isabel noisily banging her way into the store.

"Isabel!" exclaimed Karen.

"I don't believe this," said Tina in disgust.

"She's like a fungus—she's everywhere," said Mandy.

"There's a fun-gus amon-gus," said Karen. "Let's get out of here."

The Girls ran out of the store. "You chased them away," said Batty angrily, turning on Isabel.

"I didn't do anything," said Isabel, glowering at him. "I haven't seen Fitz in a long time, and he and I are going to traipse about in the woods." She gathered up Fitz's leash.

"Traipse!" Batty scoffed.

"Amble, meander, traverse," said Isabel, blazing up.

At least, Cully thought, she's beginning to stand up to him.

"Walking Fitz is Cully's job," Batty objected.

"Come on, Isabel," said Cully, taking the leash from her and clipping it onto Fitz's collar. "I'll go with you."

Out on the street Cully said, "He's mad because he was hoping to get those girls' shadows."

"Oooh! What an idea!" Isabel's eyes gleamed. "Then maybe they'd stop being so mean to me."

"They'd turn even meaner," said Cully.

Cully felt for the cloak. He was amazed how it had compressed itself into something small enough to fit in his pocket. "Listen, Isabel, I need your help. Can you distract your grandfather long enough for me to snatch the key out of his shirt pocket? I've got the spy-cloak, so he won't see me."

Isabel stopped walking. "Why?" she asked.

"I have to get into that back room you told me about." Cully studied Isabel's face and then took the plunge. "My dad's shadow is in one of the boxes back there."

Isabel's face turned red. "Ooo, that is so—so—" For once she seemed to be at a loss for words. "Don't worry, I'll think of something good."

Returning to the store, Isabel held the door open. Invisible under the cloak, Cully stepped in ahead of her. "Grandpa!" she called out. "There's something wrong with Fitz! Come quick!"

"What do you mean?" Batty hurried out from behind the counter, looking alarmed.

As he knelt down to inspect Fitz, Batty's shirt pocket billowed into the shape of a cup. Cully approached and carefully reached into the pocket, making sure his hand was concealed under the cloak. He extracted the key without disturbing the shirt at all.

Key in hand, Cully tiptoed slowly across the room, holding his breath as one of the floorboards creaked.

"I don't see anything wrong with him," said Batty.

"He was breathing funny, Grandpa," said Isabel.

Cully reached the door and slotted the key into the lock. As he turned the knob, the door opened faster than he anticipated and the black coat swooshed forward.

Out of the corner of his eye, Cully saw Batty's head jerk up.

"Must be some kind of ghost in here," said Isabel nervously.

Leaping to his feet, Batty slapped a hand against his shirt pocket. "Think I was born yesterday, do you?" he roared.

Cully slipped through the door, closing it firmly, but he

was in too much of a hurry and he didn't lock it again. In a second Batty was behind him, shouting, "Don't think you're going to get away with this!"

Cully hurtled down the aisle, but he was finding it difficult to run while keeping himself covered with the cloak. He stumbled slightly, and Batty, not seeing him, smashed into him, and they both went sprawling on the floor.

"You stupid boy," Batty gasped, and groping for Cully, shoved him hard. By the time Cully was back on his feet, Batty was holding a manila envelope up in the air.

Cully could see the big block letters: *PENNYACRE, JOHN I.*

"Come and get it," Batty taunted.

Cully stood still, trying to think. He began to move slowly toward Batty, trying not to make a sound. If he could just get close enough to reach up and grab the envelope—but Batty suddenly started rushing toward him, full throttle, and Cully was in danger of being knocked over again.

Not caring anymore whether or not he was invisible, Cully wrapped the cloak around his neck, turned, and sprinted down the aisle. He was out of the room in a flash, but the cloak caught in the door as he slammed it shut. He fumbled for the key, and the lock only just clicked into place as Batty threw his full weight against the door. The old wood cracked ominously, but it didn't give. Batty started pounding with his fists, yelling and cursing.

Isabel appeared in the hallway, her eyes wide and questioning. "Is he locked in?"

"Yes," said Cully.

"Did you get your dad's—"

Cully bit his lip in frustration. "No. He has it. In there. And the cloak is caught in the door."

They walked slowly back to the storefront.

"Now what do we do?" Isabel asked.

"I don't know," said Cully, and then his heart sank as a harried-looking Kipper came jangling into the store. Fitz yelped as she stepped on his tail.

"Give us a hand, will you?" Kipper commanded brusquely. "Mrs. Handsaker needs help getting through the door."

An older woman was sitting in a wheelchair just outside the door. She grumbled as Isabel pushed and Cully pulled. "Don't understand why that Kipper Ballou had to rush me down here like this."

"What's all that noise?" Kipper asked suddenly, her head cocked in the direction of the back room.

Cully and Isabel looked at each other. "It's Grandpa," said Isabel finally. "He locked himself in the back room by accident."

"Oh, for heaven's sakes!" Kipper exclaimed. "Why haven't you let him out?"

"We don't have the key," said Isabel.

"Don't have the—just stay right there, Mrs. Handsaker," said Kipper. "Don't go anywhere—I'll be right back." She rushed behind the counter, found a screwdriver and hammer in the clutter, and then barreled her way into the hallway to the Shadow Room. "I'm coming, Pops!" she shouted.

"What is she doing?" Mrs. Handsaker asked grumpily.

There was a loud bashing and tearing and ripping, and a moment later Batty appeared, red in the face, shaking with rage, holding the envelope. "I'm handing this over to your husband," he said to Kipper. "He'll be able to fetch the best price for it."

Cully lunged across the counter for the envelope, but

Batty tucked it behind his back. "Oh no, you don't," he growled.

"What is going on here?" asked Kipper indignantly.

"This apprentice is fired!" Batty shouted, pounding the counter with his fist.

"Are you going to fire me, too, Grandpa?" asked Isabel.

"Yes!" Batty shouted again.

"Don't be ridiculous," said Kipper. "She's your grandchild—you can't fire your grandchild."

"Good idea," Mrs. Handsaker piped up. "I'd like to fire my grandchildren—spoiled brats, if you ask me."

Batty strode out in front of the counter. "I'm taking this to Bobo right now."

"Wait a second," said Cully. His heart was beating so hard his chest hurt. "If you give it to me, I'll—I'll—"

"You'll what?" Batty sneered.

"Mrs. Ballou can have the back 40 acres of Pennyacre Farm."

"No, Cully," said Isabel in a sort of wail.

Kipper stepped forward. She seemed to swell in Cully's eyes like a balloon. "Let him have whatever it is, Pops," she said. "This is the break we've been waiting for. Apple Blossom Acres, here we come!"

"Apple Blossom Acres!" Cully gasped.

Kipper made a dramatic gesture with her hand. "About twenty cottages, I'm thinking. Apple Seed Avenue, Apple Core Lane."

"This is crazy!" Isabel cried out. "Grandpa, you have to—"

Batty turned on Isabel, furious. "You keep your mouth shut, *now*," he snarled at her. "I won't be told what to do by a child who can't even hold on to her own—"

"Stop it! Stop it!" Isabel screamed. She ran out of the store, and Fitz, who had started up from his place by the door as soon as the shouting had begun, bolted out after her.

"Fitz!" Batty roared. "Come back here! Cully, go after him."

"You fired me," said Cully.

"Oh, never mind," Batty groaned. "Fitz is a good dog—he'll come back."

Kipper put her hands on her hips. "Just what is it Isabel can't do?"

Batty gave her a look. "What do you care? You never cared before. I tried to tell you, and you wouldn't listen. You said if it had anything to do with shadows, you didn't want to know."

"And I still don't," said Kipper. "What do shadows matter now, anyway? We've got Apple Blossom Acres."

"He's just a boy," said Batty, turning away in disgust. "His word means nothing."

"We will get an agreement in writing from the Penny-acre sisters," said Kipper calmly.

Batty clutched the envelope tightly. "It better be signed, sealed, and witnessed."

"How do I know I can trust you?" Cully demanded. "*Your* word means nothing."

"Put the object in question in a safe-deposit box at the bank," said Mrs. Handsaker. Everyone turned to stare at her. "I'm a lawyer," she said, her crusty face looking cheerful for the first time, "and I can tell you, a box at the bank is the only fair way to go. You'll have a disinterested third party taking care of the object in question. No more carrying on like a pack of savages."

"Perfectly right," said Kipper happily. "So now we proceed to the bank."

"I will carry the object in question there myself," said Mrs. Handsaker crisply. She held out her hand for the envelope. "Thank you very much," she said as Batty reluctantly handed the envelope over.

"I have to stay here," said Batty grumpily, "for when Fitz comes back."

With Kipper Ballou leading the way, Cully wheeled Mrs. Handsaker down Main Street to the Medley Savings Bank. Mrs. Handsaker explained to a clerk what was needed.

When the envelope was safely locked in a box in a vault beneath the main floor of the bank, Mrs. Handsaker said to Kipper, "And now you may take me home, Mrs. Ballou."

"What about your valuable paintings?" Kipper asked. "Wouldn't you like to discuss them with Mr. Bates?"

Mrs. Handsaker smiled grimly. "I don't know how you ever suckered me into coming into that store in the first place. I will tell you again, I am not interested in selling my paintings, and I want to go home now; otherwise I'll charge you double for the trouble I've just taken. As it is, you'll get my bill in the morning."

"Wonderful," said Kipper chirpily, "and I can't thank you enough for all you've done."

"Humph," said Mrs. Handsaker.

On the way out of the bank, Cully's eye was caught by a sign on an office door: **Robert Ballou, Manager.**

And then there was Bobo himself, emerging from his office, towering over Kipper as he greeted her. "What a surprise to see you, my dear," he said. "What brings you to the bank?"

"Just a little business, Bobo," said Kipper, tugging at her jacket. Cully had the definite impression that Bobo made Kipper nervous. "I'm helping Cully put a valuable possession of his in a safe-deposit box." She gave Cully a significant look, as if to say, Let's keep this little secret between us, eh?

Cully looked from Bobo to Kipper—Bobo, the banker, and Kipper, the real-estate agent. He couldn't help believing Kipper had come sniffing after their land because Bobo had told her the Pennyacres were having trouble keeping up with their payments.

"Well, well," said Bobo, his smug face beaming. "Your valuables, whatever they are, will be safe with us."

Cully immediately had misgivings, but he had no choice but to head out. He gathered up his bike but pedaled slowly, not really wanting to go back to the farm, because once there he would have to tell his aunts what he had done.

Maybe, just maybe, he thought as he rode along, Kipper's scheme wasn't all a scam. Maybe cottages would be built, and all those old people would come to live on the farm; after all, Cully rather liked Mr. Crimps and Mr. Masumoto and Mrs. Towsley.

Cully stopped pedaling as the high school came into sight. A lot of his teammates seemed to be there, playing on the outdoor court. Cully climbed off the bike and leaned it against a tree, glad of an excuse to put off a little longer the awful moment of talking to his aunts. He'd play a little pickup game, hang out for a while. But as he approached, he was surprised to see that the boys weren't running around or setting up shots. They were standing in a circle and laughing in a loud, raucous way that sent shivers up his spine.

Archie Sticks was in the middle of the circle, and the boys

were taking turns whaling a ball at him as hard they could. Archie was tall for his age, and broad, which made him an easy target. His face was contorted with concentration as he managed to twist his body this way and that, avoiding the ball. But Cully's appearance distracted him, and as Will Suitor flung the ball, it caught Archie hard in the middle.

"Bingo!" Will crowed as Archie doubled over with a gasp.

Cully couldn't believe his eyes. These guys could rag on you, but normally they weren't bullies. Now every single boy had a strange expression on his face—a mean look Cully had never seen before.

The reason for it was starkly apparent: the fence, the basketball hoop, the trees growing nearby all cast a network of shadows on the surface of the court, and yet, like Archie, every single boy was shadowless.

"Hey, Cull!" Nick Slater cried out. "We went into Batty's Attic looking for you. Why didn't you tell us what a cool store it is? And that Batty guy, he's got this funky hobby!"

Archie, meanwhile, was taking advantage of the fact that the boys had forgotten him for a moment. He began edging toward a slight gap in the circle.

"Oh no, you don't!" yelled Ned Handy. "Where do you think you're going, Archie Stinks?"

The boys guffawed. "Archie Stinks! That's a good one!"

"Archie has to go," said Cully, thinking quickly. "I've been looking all over for him. Coach Stevens wants to meet with him."

Will looked disbelieving. "Coach wants to meet with *Archie*?"

Cully improvised. "Coach is over at Pete's right now,

waiting for you, Archie. He wants you back on the team. You better hustle."

Archie darted free of the circle like a terrified rabbit escaping a ring of jackals. As soon as he was at a safe distance he shouted, "I wouldn't go back on that dumb team if you gave me a million dollars!" And then he ran for all he was worth.

Cully groaned. So much for saving Archie's skin.

"Hey, Pennyacre, maybe you like that jerk more than us," said Ned.

The boys started running up the slight hill Cully was standing on.

"Maybe you'd like to take his place in the middle," Will said menacingly.

"Not today," said Cully. He forced himself to walk, not run. He gathered up his bike. "So long, guys," he said, taking off as the group surged toward him.

Pedaling furiously along Route 5, Cully finally understood why Batty wanted him as an apprentice. He was shadow bait. Batty was counting on him to bring kids into the store. And because of him, Cully thought with an increasingly sick feeling in the pit of his stomach, Batty now had a basketball team's worth of young shadows.

As Cully put his bike away he saw the aunts sitting out on the porch, Scooter next to Inca on the swing seat, looking as if he had lived at Pennyacre Farm all his life. As Cully approached he heard Miggs telling a story about Kipper Ballou in a loud voice, punctuated with great peals of laughter. He caught the tail end of the tale—"and she actually thought she could get away with building storage units on our property!"

"*Storage units,*" Inca exploded.

"Now I'm *really* glad we didn't give in to her pressure to sell," said Opal in an outraged tone of voice.

Cully gripped the porch railing. He thought he was going to either faint or get sick. He sat down abruptly on the bottom step.

"What's the matter, Cully?" Inca asked. "You're looking mighty pale."

"Hey, buddy, what's up?" Scooter came over to the stairs and sat beside Cully.

Cully shook his head. He couldn't speak.

"I'm having trouble making the apple fuel work," Scooter said to him. "I feel as if something important has been left out of your dad's Recipe."

"I don't know what it could be," Cully mumbled.

Cully got up and walked around to the back of the house and looked up at the hill. The tall pine tree stood out, a sentry guarding the woods behind. Pink clouds gathered in the sky. As the evening star appeared, the sky turned from pink to lavender to inky blue to black. He felt, as much as saw, the solid form of the hill and the rock it was made of. He sensed the creatures who lived in the woods: the owls and squirrels, the mice, the snakes, the bobcat, the deer. There were also foxes, hawks, and even wood-boring insects grinding away at the fallen and decaying tree trunks.

As he looked around at the apple trees, Cully remembered Grandpa Will saying how much he loved the combination of tamed orchard and wild woods. He tried not to picture the hill stripped of trees, with aluminum sheds glinting in the sun.

"The land is still here, right now," he said. He breathed deeply, as if his blood cells could be made to memorize his land by the oxygen he breathed into them.

Inca and Scooter were walking in the orchard now, arm in arm, fireflies flickering about them. Cully thought with alarm that he had better get to the aunts before Kipper did. He wished Inca were not so happy with Scooter at this moment—she would have been the easiest to approach first.

Cully turned and went into the house. He paused for a moment in the mudroom, looking into the big, old kitchen. Opal was inside now, sitting at her roll-top desk. She looked thinner than ever and was wearing dark colors as usual. In his heart of hearts, he'd always been a little afraid of her. She was a serious person, always dealing with numbers and taxes and the cost of things. But now Cully felt a surge of sympathy for her. He realized how hard she had worked since his grandparents' death to hold the farm together.

Still, he didn't have the nerve to tell her the news. He tiptoed past Opal and climbed the stairs to the middle floor. Miggs was sitting at her kitchen table poring over farm machinery catalogs.

"Hi, Cully!" she said without looking up.

Cully stood near her without answering.

"Something on your mind?" she asked, still not looking up.

"Oh, nothing, really," said Cully, his voice tight. He didn't know how to broach the subject.

Miggs looked up, studying Cully's face. "Well, tell me

about nothing, then." She pushed the catalogs away. "It's not every night you want to talk to me about nothing."

She went over to refrigerator and took out a bottle of milk and poured two glasses. She carried them and a plate of gingersnaps over to the table and sat down.

"Sit," she said.

Cully slowly went over and sat down. "I did a terrible thing today," he said.

Miggs smiled. "How terrible could it be?"

"The most terrible thing you could imagine—" Cully gulped slightly and then went on. "I made a bargain with Kipper Ballou—I said she could have the back 40 acres—if—if—they would keep dad safe."

Miggs's forehead furrowed with confusion. "*They?*"

"Kipper and Batty."

"I don't understand," said Miggs. "What have Kipper and Batty to do with Jack?"

Cully struggled. "I don't know how to explain this—"

"You can't *possibly* have made such a bargain with Kipper Ballou," Miggs said, scraping back her chair and standing up. Her sunburned face was creased with worry. "It's just not possible."

Cully clenched his fists, trying to hold himself together. "I had to—I couldn't think of any other way."

Miggs hitched her thumbs into her overall straps. "I think," she said finally, "that I'm calling a meeting."

There was an ancient phone system rigged up between floors. Using a hand crank, Miggs rang once for Opal. "Meeting in the middle," she said. She rang three times for Inca.

"Inca's in the orchard," said Cully.

Miggs put down the phone and pushed up a window and

140

stuck her head outside. "Inca," she shouted. "I'm calling a meeting. Right now. And no Scooter, please."

Cully sat at the table, almost paralyzed with misery.

"What's going on?" Opal asked, looking faintly annoyed as she came in.

Inca followed. "What's happened?" she asked.

"Come and sit down," said Miggs.

Opal and Inca sat down. Miggs remained standing.

"Cully was telling me some—um—interesting—news about—um—Kipper Ballou," said Miggs. She folded her arms across her chest. "Cully? I think you should try to explain."

Cully closed his eyes for a moment and pressed his fingers to his eyelids. He felt sick and dizzy.

"Cully?" Inca reached over and put a hand on his shoulder. Her touch was warm and comforting, and it gave him courage. He opened his eyes and took a breath.

"Batty has this hobby," Cully began. "He collects shadows. He has this *contraption*—it's in a room behind the store." Step by step, Cully went on to describe shadow-collecting. Opal and Miggs listened with expressions of disbelief. He went on to explain Kipper Ballou's Apple Blossom Acres scheme. "And Batty somehow got—Dad's shadow." He rushed the words out. "If we give Kipper our land for her cottages— for her storage sheds—Batty won't sell Dad's shadow. We can save it from being turned into a spy-cloak."

Both Miggs and Opal exploded, but Inca sat without saying a word, her eyes huge.

"Oh, poor sweetie," said Opal, shaking her head in sorrow as she looked at Cully. "Jack's disappearance has weighed on you more than you ever let on."

"I've been working you too hard," said Miggs, brushing tears away with the back of her hand.

"Stop it," said Inca. Everyone turned to stare at her. Inca normally never sounded cross. "You're acting as if he's lost his mind, and he hasn't. You *know* Jack worked in intelligence when he was in the military. I used to think he was joking when he said shadows was his line of work—but now I see that's exactly what it was."

Miggs groaned. "That was a *code* name, Inca. He never *literally* worked with shadows."

"That's all you know, and Batty *is* taking people's shadows," Inca retorted. "Ask Scooter if you don't believe us."

"Check out Mr. Masumoto the next time he comes to the farm," said Cully. "He doesn't have a shadow anymore, and I'm telling you, he acts different now. There are others, too— Archie Sticks, Mr. Crimps, Mrs. Towsley, the kids on my team. They all act different now, and what it means is, *Dad* is different, too. It's what made him leave us—and now he's a million miles away in Japan, and Kipper Ballou is going to take over our property, and there's nothing we can do about any of it." Cully bowed his head, willing himself not to cry.

Miggs started pacing. Inca played with the salt and pepper shakers on the table. Opal sat completely still and then, tucking a strand of white hair behind an ear, said, "I don't understand the part about the shadows, but I do know that Jack's welfare is more important than 40 acres of land. Cully, you did absolutely the right thing."

Miggs stopped pacing for a moment. "I don't understand the shadow stuff either, but I do know we are not going to let that Ballou woman get the best of us." She pulled up a chair and sat down. "Listen, she can't make this happen overnight.

They have to survey boundaries and get lawyers to draw up agreements. In the meantime, maybe we can—maybe we can—"

"—make Leapin' Lizzie leap," said Inca, rising to her feet. "And then we'll make a fortune selling apple fuel, just as Jack always intended. Scooter can help us, I know he can. And then we can afford to buy Kipper out."

"I don't know—" said Opal.

"Maybe—" said Miggs.

Cully looked from one aunt to the other. They weren't blaming him for anything. He no longer had to go through this nightmare alone. And maybe—just maybe—Jack's Recipe *would* pull them through. Cully drank the milk and ate the gingersnaps, feeling comforted to the marrow of his bones.

When Cully finally closed his eyes that night, he felt himself being pulled into the dark again. Then came the squishing and the squashing, and he knew he was being turned into a lightow.

Opening his eyes, he found himself outside. His personage was standing next to a tree. Cully recognized the maple tree. Its bare branches etched fine, dark lines into an ashen sky. "Uoy tsum nepo eht rood," said his shadow.

12

When Cully woke up he immediately went downstairs and out into the yard and stood before the maple tree. In the early morning light the bright green leaves of all the other trees around him struck him as beautiful, and in contrast the maple tree seemed even more barren than usual.

What was it Inca was always saying—that the tree was waiting for Jack to come home? Or was Miggs right when she said the tree had leaf scorch or root rot? The aunts were going to wait a season to see if the leaves came back, and if not the tree would get cut down.

But Cully was standing there in front of the maple now because of the words his shadow had spoken to him in the dream; in its backward shadow language it had said, *You must open the door.*

There was only one door that he knew of. Cully knelt down. The roots were exposed at the base of the trunk, and a long time ago Jack had made a door to fit against one of the hollow spaces between the roots. He had called it a house for a mouse, and had even hung a tiny wreath on the door at Christmastime.

Cully opened the door and saw the wooden box his father still kept in the Mouse House. He knew, without looking, that the box contained a snake skin, a piece of rose quartz, a mouse skull, a photograph of his mother, two small blue jay feathers, a turkey vulture feather, a quail's feather, and an ancient Coca-Cola bottle cap.

A little fur of moss was growing on the outside of the box. It had been awhile since anyone had touched it. Opening it now, Cully found the old treasures but also something he had never seen before: a small book bound in brown leather. Page after page was filled with his father's scrawl. Unable to help himself, he started reading right at the beginning.

April 2, 1962. Have this idea for developing a fuel that's not based on petroleum or gasoline. Tanks in the army ran on biodiesel fuel, so why can't everyday vehicles do so as well? I will need to convert Lizzie's engine and rig it up with a special fuel pump, among many other things.

May 24. Today I thought: APPLES. Why not? Perfect way to use up our drops.

Possible Problems: Increased dilution and polymerization of engine sump oil; pump seizures; high fuel viscosity. How will fuel function in winter? Maybe too cold?

June 6. New second-hand/antique store in town called Batty's Attic. Run by an eccentric old guy named Jim Bates. It's also a pawn shop. Got me thinking: I could use a little extra cash right now to set up a lab to make fuel in the barn.

June 8. Building a darkroom for Jim Bates. Putting in sink and shelves and running water for him. In return he's giving me some glass flasks, tubing, and several old barrels. My lab is a little primitive so far, but it's a start.

June 10. Helped Batty install a clunky old apparatus in his darkroom today. I swear the contraption looks just like one of those old World War I stripping doodads—I'd say it is a 1916 model. Special beam stimulates the molecules, which leads to spontaneous separation as long as you also paint the image with photonic chemicals. Couldn't help asking Batty if he knew what he had. Batty acted as if he had no idea what I was talking about—said it was just part of his camera equipment.

Would love to have a chance to look at the apparatus again, but Batty says darkroom is all set. I might be imagining it, but he sure seems reluctant to have me go back in there.

June 12. Ran into Cindy Rogers, the nice real-estate agent in town who helped Mom and Dad buy that piece of land across the highway. She was just coming out of Batty's Attic. I guess I hadn't seen her in a while—I almost didn't recognize her. She's aged so, and looks—well, her expression reminded me of expressions I used to see on some of the faces of stripped subjects—

Jumping Jehoshaphat! I just made the connection: Batty's contraption?? What am I thinking? That's ridiculous. Batty doesn't seem the type.

June 13. In town last night. Saw Cindy Rogers walking down Main Street. Saw her under the lamplight, and—I almost hate to write it—she's been stripped! I tried talking to her. She mumbled something about not feeling well, and that it was time to retire. I feel truly sick about this. Why on earth would Jim Bates be collecting shadows? Shadow-collecting is a tool of war, not of peace-loving citizens.

If that isn't bad enough, Opal called a meeting in the middle tonight. Financial problems. Opal is worried, I know, but it comes out as anger at me. "Stop messing around with mashed-up apples," she said, "and use your chemical engineering skills to make a living." I begged her to be patient. I'm close to making the fuel work; I know I am.

June 14: I was tinkering with the Recipe again tonight (yes, I'm calling it the Recipe), and by gum, I nailed it! Leapin' Lizzie was sure enough leapin' tonight! We went all the way to the coast and back. Even Opal was excited! What a wonderful way to celebrate Cully's birthday!

Oh, how I wish Tabitha could see Cully now. He's so balanced, and to tell the truth, I could use a little of his easygoing ways. Been awful worried lately about—about any number of things.

What Jim Bates is up to, for one thing.

Lovely full moon tonight. The June moon is the Strawberry Moon, an enchanting, magical moon, with shadows dancing everywhere. Oh, *shadows*. I don't want to think about them. Poor Cindy Rogers. Earlier this evening, I reminded myself I must pay a call on her—bring the naphthalene—although I have no idea, of course, where her shadow might be at this point.

But now, today, in this moment, I need to celebrate.

I have a fine son, and I've made a new kind of fuel out of apples! I have to fine-tune the Recipe, of course, so others can use it, but what a breakthrough! There is sure to be financial gain from this!

Cully felt his ears turn red as he read his father's entry about himself. But he also felt amazed as he read about Batty and Cindy Rogers. His father *knew* that Batty was shadow-collecting!

Cully turned more pages, finding more scribbles about the apple fuel recipe. Then there was another entry about Cindy Rogers.

June 16, 1962. Ran into Cindy again. Oddest thing. We were standing outside Pete's Parlor, and I saw Cindy's shadow, just as clear and dark as mine. She looked fine, too. Did I just *imagine* she had lost her shadow? I asked her if she was still going to retire, and she said not likely, not with Kipper Ballou moving into town. Cindy lowered her voice a bit and said she didn't like the way Kipper was buying up so much farmland in the area.

And then I had this sort of—*experience*. Out of the corner of my eye I thought I saw a movement, and then I saw my shadow reach out and shake Cindy's shadow's hand. I have never witnessed anything like this before, not even when I was dealing with shadow factors in the military.

Who knows—maybe my mind is playing tricks on me—I do feel under a strain. We (Opal, Miggs, Inca, and I) went to the bank to sign papers for a mortgage. Hate getting us burdened with payments every month. When Mother and Dad left us the farm it was free and clear, but there have been too many bills lately, too many repairs, and Miggs is thinking we need to modernize some of the equipment if apple farming is to turn a profit. If only I could get my Recipe to work consistently—

Pete Hamill, the banker we usually deal with, was indisposed. We worked with a new guy at the bank, Kipper Ballou's husband, Robert Ballou. Don't know why, but the guy seemed like a bully, not a guy you felt good entrusting your finances to.

Cully stopped reading for a moment, his stomach churning. Here was proof that Bobo Ballou did know about his family's financial problems.

June 18. Sometimes I wonder why I walked away from a career in intelligence. Or in chemistry. I could have been a spy, or I could have been high up in the ranks of one of those big chemical corporations. Either way I wouldn't be worried about money now, and I'd be able to travel. Time was when I wanted to see the world. Now I don't think I'll be able to.

But the up side is, if I were working my tail off and traveling all the time I wouldn't be able to see Cully every day, go fishing and canoeing with him, teach him how to be an apple farmer.

And why am I being so down on myself? I'm going to make a fortune with that fuel! I just have to be persistent.

June 19. Saw Pete Hamill and his wife, Millie, walking down Main Street, looking like they'd been hit with a Mack truck. Right away Millie told me Pete had lost his job—had been making too many mistakes lately and the bank let him go. Pete had that <u>look</u> on his face. And sure enough, he doesn't have a shadow.

Criminy, this is serious!

June 20. Made some phone calls today. Buddy of mine who works for the CIA is going to do some investigating of Mr. James Bates. Then I asked him if there's been any progress in the field of remigration. He said no, unfortunately the process still requires naphthalene.

Even when I was working in Intelligence myself, I kept hoping I'd be able to come up with a practical way of remigrating stripped subjects. The problem with the current method is you have to have access to the shadow. And right now I have no idea where Batty keeps the shadows he's been collecting.

June 24. My buddy called back. He confirmed there was a James Bates who worked in umbrage during WWI. As a matter of fact, he was quite famous in the field. He was known as "Shadowman," and because of his work we were able to obtain important secrets from the enemy. So, once upon a time, Batty was a hero.

My buddy also told me that on account of the Cold War, shadow-collecting is on the rise. In some cases the government is even turning a blind eye to illegal activities because the spy-cloaks made from shadows are so effective for gathering information.

He said I could contact the Agency Against Shadow-Collecting and tip them off as to what Batty has been up to, but he warned me they might be "hands-off" because he is a hero. Who would have thought good old Medley would become home to "Shadowman"?

But I am also thinking how best to confront Batty myself. I want to stop him, but I sense he is, well, batty, and I think he could be dangerous. I'm guessing his shadow is loose. Can't trust folks like that. I just hope it's loose and not actually frozen. When you see someone with a frozen shadow, you know you're in trouble.

Another problem: my Recipe is missing an ingredient. I haven't been able to get Lizzie running since the night of Cully's birthday, and Opal is getting on my case again.

June 26. Ran into Cindy Rogers. Holy cow! Her shadow reached out to shake my shadow's hand again. There is some kind of connection between us—

Trying to think—I saw Cindy the night before Cully's b'day and she didn't have a shadow. And the night after, she did.

Well, think, Jack—what could it be?

September 17. Full moon again. September moon is the Corn Moon. As I was tinkering with the Recipe again tonight, I found myself reciting a poem Tabitha liked— "Moonlit Apples," by John Drinkwater. Seemed appropriate, somehow, and there's that lovely line: "and the moon again / Dapples the apples with deep-sea light."

Ah, I miss Tabitha.

But here is the good news: I got Lizzie running again!

September 20. Thought I'd stop by Pete's and check up on him. Pete was outside digging in his garden, and—

good gravy!! He has a shadow again! Then Pete told me he'd had a bad spell there for a while—his doctor couldn't figure out what was wrong with him, but thank goodness, he's feeling like himself again. It is too late for Pete to get his job back at the bank, but he says he's ready to move on and try something different, anyhow. Too bad—it means we're stuck with that Ballou person.

But here's the thing that I'm finding almost impossible to take in: While Pete was talking, his shadow's hand reached over and shook my shadow's hand. It absolutely floored me! So I called my buddy at the CIA again and told him about it. He said he'd never heard of such a thing—he actually had a hard time not laughing, I could hear it in his voice. Well, I know I didn't imagine it, and it must mean something.

September 21. An amazing idea occurred to me tonight. Sort of can't believe it, but if I learned anything while I was working with shadows in the army, it was that there are all *sorts* of things in this world that are surprising. I'm going to test my theory out.

September 23: Yes! Good news! I did it! Got Leapin' Lizzie working again! Think I know what the missing ingredient is. Going to make a few more batches of the Recipe and keep testing my theory.

December 26. Saw my old English teacher, Miss Clover, coming out of Batty's. It was horrifying. She's been stripped! I was so angry, I marched right into the store and right up to Batty. "Okay, Shadowman, what's the story here?"

Batty was so startled I thought he was going to jump right out of his skin, but he quickly put a finger to his lips and glanced toward the back of the room. Our new banker, Bobo Ballou, was standing there, sort of lurking in the—well—shadows. I told Batty I'd be back.

December 27. Returned to Batty's. Made sure no one was around this time. "I'm on to you," I said, not beating about the bush. "Used to work in umbriage myself during the Korean War."

Then Batty had me sit down, and he told me the whole sorry tale. After World War I he continued working for the military for a while, but then he lost his job when shadow-collecting was made illegal. He wasn't trained to do anything else, and he wasn't quite sure what to do with himself. His wife was running an antique business, and as Batty had always been interested in old things, they decided they'd run the business together. Well, that was all fine for a while, but then Batty lost his wife, his son, and his daughter-in-law all at once in a tragic train wreck (same one, by a curious coincidence, that Melvin died in), and he now had a business to run by himself. His surviving daughter, Kipper, and her husband, Bobo, jumped in to help him out, and they also adopted the orphaned Isabel.

Still, Batty was having trouble making ends meet. "I have a good eye for antiques," he said, "but I'm not a businessman." One day in his antique hunting he came across an old shadow-maker. Batty was sure the person who sold it to him had no idea what it was, but he, of course, did know, and that's when he decided he'd make a little extra money on the side. He knew there was still a market for shadows because the Cold War was heating up.

"I don't collect shadows often," he said. "Just now and then when there's a financial gap, don't you know."

I was absolutely thunderstruck—I couldn't believe it. The man is batty, all right—stark, raving bats! "How in the world do you rationalize taking shadows from ordinary citizens?" I asked. "From people like Cindy Rogers and Pete Hamill and poor old Berenice Clover? What have they ever done to you?"

"Look," he said, "the people you just mentioned—they're getting on in life. They're at the end of things, you know? They're already forgetful, or cranky, or set in their ways. Losing their shadows doesn't affect 'em that much. I'd never take a young person's shadow—that's just plain wrong, and it always has been. And I'll tell you something else: my old machine isn't even working anymore. The last few times I've collected a shadow, it ended up remigrating. I don't know if there is a loose connection, or what. So don't report me," he said pathetically. "If you report me—well, my granddaughter, Isabel—she looks up to me—I—just don't want her knowing about this."

By this time I was shaking with rage. "If I find out one more shadow has been stripped in this town, I swear to God, AASC'll be on you in a heartbeat."

Of course I checked out Batty's shadow right then and there with my umbrage-meter (still have the one I carried around with me in the army), and believe it or not he does have a shadow, but talk about a loose connection! You better believe I'm going to keep a close eye on him.

But I was interested to hear he has also noticed that the stripped shadows are remigrating. Gosh—what if I could discover how it's happening! What an advancement that would be in the field of umbriage. Well, I just have to keep pursuing ideas, no matter how far-fetched they might seem to other people.

January 16: Big news: I've tested my theory for six full moons now. Seven, if you include June. I am convinced I have finally found the key. What a breakthrough! So many people will benefit! And here it is—I'm writing it down, just in case anything happens to me.

Reciting a poem you've memorized, under a full moon.

And that was the last entry.

"That's ridiculous!" Cully burst out. "You can't make a truck run by reciting a poem under a full moon."

13

"Oh my word!" Inca exclaimed as she read Jack's diary. Cully had brought it up to the Tower Room and was looking through the Chest of Moths while she read it. "All that time, Jack knew what Batty was up to—"

"Knock knock," said Scooter, his head appearing in the doorway.

"How's the fuel coming along, Scooter?"

Scooter drew his dark eyebrows together. "If this whole thing doesn't work because of me—" His hair was a mess, he had circles under his eyes, and his fingers were black with grease.

"Oh, Scooter, don't be silly," said Inca without looking up from the diary, "you can do this, you really can."

"The Recipe is not working. I've followed every darn direction Jack wrote down," he said. "Every darn equation—"

Inca looked up. "Maybe you haven't," she said. She got up from her desk and went over to the wall where a calendar was hanging. "Full moon coming up. How quickly can you memorize a poem?"

Scooter looked aghast. "I never could! They always made us memorize poems in school, and I always froze up. And anyway, what are you talking about?"

Inca held up the little brown diary. "Jack wrote here that

the key is reciting a poem you've memorized under a full moon." She pointed to the entry and held it under Scooter's nose. "He says so right here."

"Oh, Inca, come on!" Cully burst out.

Ignoring him, Inca pulled back her hair and twisted and piled it up on top of her head. "You've tried everything else, Scooter; we owe it to Jack to give this a try."

Scooter read the diary entry and then handed the book back to Inca. "Good chance he already lost his shadow by the time he wrote this," he said, shaking his head.

"That's what I'm worried about," said Cully. "It's not reliable—it's—"

"Did he or did he not get the fuel to work the night of your birthday, when there was a full moon?" Inca asked Cully. "Did he or did he not recite 'Birches' as he was filling the tank? And look," she said, finding the page in the diary and jabbing a finger at it, "he recited the apple poem on the night of another full moon when he was filling the tank." Inca pinned Cully with one of her most intense looks.

Cully rose to his feet, pushing the drawers back into the Chest. He knew Inca would not give up on this idea. "So who's going to do the memorizing?" he asked.

"All of us," said Inca. "We want to make sure it works."

Every spring after the blossoms fell off the apple trees, little apples started forming, growing in clusters. And every spring Miggs and Cully went around to each cluster, pulling off the little apples, leaving only one in each cluster so that it could grow up to be big and healthy. It was also important not to let two apples grow side by side, because if they touched they could spread diseases. This process was called *culling*.

Miggs always said Cully had agile fingers, a knack for culling. "And that's why," she liked to tease him, "we named you Cully!"

Cully and Miggs were in the orchard now, up on ladders, fingers busily pulling away little apples. Miggs was carrying on as if life were normal. It was her way, Cully knew, of dealing with stress. He also knew Miggs believed hard work was the answer to everything—if only the Pennyacres worked hard enough, Kipper could do them no harm.

"Cully!"

As Cully looked down he saw Isabel, her little face beaming up at him. She was wearing a pink leotard and tights and pink ballet slippers.

"I came straight from ballet, but I wanted to show you something," Isabel said, holding up a large book.

"What?" he grunted, but he was relieved to see that she seemed to be all right. He had been wondering what had happened to her after she stormed out of Batty's.

"Come down from there and I'll show you," she said.

"I don't know if I can," he said. "We're culling, and it has to be done now or it'll affect the harvest."

"I'll help you after you look at this."

"I don't know—culling is careful work," Cully said, wiping the sweat off his face, "and boring and tiring."

"Will you stop flapping that trap of yours and come down here and take a look?" said Isabel. "It's important."

Cully was actually glad to have an excuse to stop for a few minutes. He climbed down the ladder.

"Your orchard smells good," said Isabel. She was standing in a bunch of clover, holding the book. "I've just spent the night with Mrs. Towsley."

"Mrs. Towsley?" Cully squinted at Isabel in a puzzled way as he squatted down beside her.

"When I left the store I saw Fitz come running after me, so I held on to his collar and we went into the woods, and I sat there and cried, and Fitz licked my face, and I decided I wasn't going back home for a while. And then I realized I was sitting right by that stump where I'd stashed Mrs. Towsley's box. I had this moment of panic—what if someone found the box—but it was there, all fine and everything, so I picked it up and Fitz and I walked over to Mrs. Towsley's store. I told her I was giving the collection back to her. Her eyes got big and she said wasn't I the sweetest girl in the world, and she gave me this huge hug, and then she said, 'But you've been crying,' and she invited me and Fitz to come up to her apartment for some tea, and we ended up talking for a long time and I ended up staying there. But, Cully, I came here to tell you something else." Isabel lowered her voice and grabbed Cully's arm. "Her shadow didn't separate."

Startled, Cully sat squarely down on the ground next to Isabel. "Are you sure?"

Isabel let go of Cully's arm. "Well, yes, I saw her shadow plain as day. And she doesn't act at all—that *way*. She kept asking me all these questions, like what Grandpa does with the shadows. I felt like a traitor, but I told her everything I know." She narrowed her eyes and pulled her mouth into a tight, straight line. "You know what?" she said after a moment, "I don't even care if Grandpa gets into trouble." She was quiet again, and Cully didn't know what to say. He certainly didn't blame Isabel for being so mad at Batty. Then Isabel shifted and pointed to the book she had placed across her knees. "I want to show you this book. It belongs to Mrs. Towsley, but she said I could borrow it for a while."

Isabel held the book so Cully could read the title. "*Shadows and Their Properties: Published and Updated Annually by the Agency Against Shadow Collectors,*" Cully read slowly. "Holy smokes," he added. "*Mrs. Towsley* had this?"

"Listen to this." Isabel opened the book and read, " 'Even when shadow-collecting was legal, collecting shadows of twelve- to sixteen-year-olds was always against the law, although from 1840 to 1914, shadow-collecting was often used as a means of recruiting child labor during the Industrial Revolution.' And there's more." She flipped through a few more pages. " '*Umbrosity* is the condition wherein the subject's shadow cannot, or will not, part. Children are *umbrose* until the age of twelve. After that, the bonds between most people and their shadows loosen to some extent; however, there are exceptions. *Umbrosity* after the age of twelve is seen in a person who has suffered a loss of a parent at an early age but who has then been truly loved and cared for by the remaining parent and/or by a foster parent or other members of the family, such as aunts, uncles, or grandparents. The shadow of an *umbrose* person will not ever separate.' " Isabel stopped reading. Then she said, "That's *you*, all right, Cully. And," she added bleakly, "I guess no one ever loved *me* enough. I mean, I know Kipper did try, but I guess she didn't really know how, and I'm pretty sure Batty used to—but—"

Isabel broke off, and Cully thought it would be better not to look at her face right at that moment; he grabbed the book out of her hands and flipped to the table of contents. "What about getting a shadow to come back?" he asked.

"I was getting to that," said Isabel, sniffing slightly and

rubbing at her eyes with the back of one hand. "Look on page 61. But be careful, will you? You're gonna rip Mrs. Towsley's book."

"'Remigration of Shadows,'" Cully read, having turned the pages as quickly as he could. And he remembered—*remigration* was the word his father had used a few times in his diary.

"'*Remigration*: the act of a shadow returning to its owner,'" Cully read. "'Remigration is achieved by placing a shadow in close proximity to naphthalene. Over the course of two to three days, the chemical compound naphthalene will stimulate a reaction in the shadow, causing it to seek rebondage with it original owner. Naphthalene is the only chemical substance known to cause this reaction.'"

Cully realized he had also encountered that strange word, *naphthalene*, in his father's diary.

"You could take a bunch of naph-whatever-it-is and put it in the envelope with your dad's shadow," said Isabel excitedly. "You just have to be able to get the—but oh my gosh!" Isabel stopped talking and stared at Cully with wide eyes. "I can't believe I didn't even ask you. What happened yesterday after I left?" She hunched her shoulders slightly, as if afraid of the answer. "Is your father's shadow—is it—"

"Dad's shadow is at the bank in a safe-deposit box," said Cully, and he told Isabel how Mrs. Handsaker had come up with the idea.

Isabel scrambled to her feet. "Then you have to go and put the naph stuff in the box at the bank."

"I don't have the slightest idea what naph—tha—lene is, and I can barely even say it," Cully said, shutting the book and slowly getting to his feet, too.

"What's the story here, Cully?" Miggs asked, walking by with a ladder. She was wearing a red bandana and her cheeks were as red and shiny as an apple's. "We have to keep at this."

"Have you ever heard of something called naphthalene?" Cully asked her.

Miggs pulled off her bandana and wiped her face with it. She frowned as she tried to think. "Naphthalene," she repeated. "Well, it's a chemical in mothballs."

Cully leaped into the air. "Mothballs!" he shouted.

Isabel ran to Miggs. "Please show me how to do that culling thing," she said. "Cully has to go into town." Isabel ran back to Cully and nudged him with her elbow. "You can go and put mothballs in the safe-deposit box right now."

Cully nodded. "I'll be gone for just an hour, Miggs," he said. "It's something really, really important I have to do— it's going to help Dad—and I'll tell you about it later," he added, not wanting to tell Miggs at all, knowing she had her doubts about shadows in general. "I know Isabel will be good at culling. She's good at everything."

"Well," said Miggs, "if it's to help Jack—" But she frowned at Isabel. "You can't work in that outfit," she said. "Better come into the house and I'll find you something more suitable."

"Miggs," said Inca, coming out into the orchard, "have you decided which poem you're going to memorize?"

"Ode to Mothballs," said Miggs rudely, turning her back on Inca.

Not wanting to hear the continuing fight between Inca and Miggs over Jack's Recipe, Cully sprinted the distance from the middle of the orchard to the house. The mothballs were kept in the little cupboard under the stairs along with other poisonous things like rat poison and weed killer. The latch to the cupboard was stiff, and Cully's fingers were slippery with sweat. He stretched out his T-shirt to get a grip, and finally managed to open the little door.

Grabbing up the box of mothballs, Cully looked around for something to put them in. He couldn't just march into the bank and say he wanted to put a bunch of mothballs in a safe-deposit box—at least he didn't think he could. Then he remembered his father's treasure box.

Cully ran outside and, kneeling at the foot of the maple tree, opened the door of the Mouse House and brought out the box. He carefully took out the treasures. He wished he knew exactly how many mothballs to put in, but he poured them into the box until they covered the bottom. They looked like small, white marbles. He replaced the treasures on top of them and went into the mudroom in search of a backpack.

Isabel and Miggs were just coming downstairs. "You're still here? You better hurry up!" said Isabel. She was wearing a pair of overalls and a red bandana. Judging by the patches, the overalls were an old pair from when Miggs was a girl. Isabel looked like Miggs Junior.

Cully hopped onto his bike and began pedaling as fast as he could. His heart sank as he came down Main Street. He couldn't believe his bad luck: Bobo and Kipper Ballou and Batty were all standing outside the bank on the sidewalk. They seemed to be shouting at each other. Cully's first impulse was to turn around and run, but Kipper had already spotted him.

"Cully Pennyacre, have you seen Isabel?"

Cully slung the backpack reluctantly over one shoulder as he approached the three adults. With a jolt he noticed there were three people standing in the sun, but there were only two shadows.

Cully looked again, wanting to be sure. Bobo and Kipper were standing close together, their shadows overlapping, but there were two shadows, no question. Batty stood with his feet planted squarely on the sidewalk, but no dark form extended from him. The concrete he was standing on looked too bright. *Amputation* was the word that floated into Cully's mind—as if some vital part of Batty were missing.

"Cully Pennyacre, didn't you hear me?" Kipper was rasping at him again, tugging at her suit jacket. "Have you seen or talked to Isabel? I know you two are as thick as thieves. Pops hurt her feelings, and she ran away to Leona Towsley, of all people! I want you to go and talk to her. Please," she added, almost tearfully. "I have been so worried."

Cully merely shook his head, muttering, "I doubt she'd listen to me."

"She isn't listening to anyone," said Bobo. "Imagine! An eleven-year-old girl controlling us like this! If we let her get away with this outrageous behavior, we'll have nothing but trouble from now on."

Bobo was wagging a scolding finger at Kipper, shifting from foot to foot in an agitated sort of way. Cully gradually realized with horror that Bobo's shadow was not shifting with him, nor was his shadow finger wagging at Kipper. Bobo's shadow arms and hands remained hanging by his shadow sides.

"Pops, you better go over to that Towsley woman's house right now," said Kipper, turning to face Batty. Her shadow turned with her, and Cully thought it seemed faintly blue, the color lightows turned when they were sad or upset. "You caused this."

"I *did* go," said Batty. "Fitz wouldn't let me in the door. He stood there growling and snapping. *Fitz!*"

Bobo grunted in response and shook his head, but his shadow's head didn't move. *At all.*

When you see someone with a frozen shadow, Jack had written in his diary, *you know you're in trouble.*

Cully only just managed to remember what he was there to do. He pulled the box out of the backpack. "I want to know if it's okay to put my treasure box in the bank with the—with the envelope." His voice came out as a croak. "I want to keep my treasures safe."

"Treasures, eh? Let's take a look," said Bobo.

Trying to keep his hands steady, Cully opened the box. He prayed being outside would help disperse the smell of the mothballs. Bobo started poking through the treasures with a pen he was holding. His shadow's hand continued to hang by his side. "I see you have marbles in there," he said. "A collection, is it?"

Heart pounding, Cully pulled out the cat's-eye marble, which, luckily, was still in the pocket of his jeans. "I almost forgot—I'm putting my best marble in there, too."

"Ah, yes, the cat's-eye," said Batty. "Good idea. It *is* valuable."

"Well, go on in and ask the clerk for the key," said Bobo.

"Yes," said Batty, "hurry up, lock up those treasures, keep them safe!"

As the clerk gave Cully the key and respectfully stood outside the vault as Cully opened the box, he couldn't resist looking inside the envelope. The shadow was in there, folded up neatly like a letter waiting to be mailed. It was all he could do not to snatch it away.

Just a few days, Cully thought as he rode home. That's all we need.

Isabel and Miggs were at work, up on ladders, when Cully arrived home. "You were right about this girl," Miggs called down to Cully. "She caught on right away, and she's quick."

Isabel beamed, and her fingers flew through the clusters even faster. Miggs climbed down and moved her ladder to another tree.

Cully leaned his ladder right beside Isabel's and climbed up. "I did it," he said. "I put the mothballs in, but Isabel, did you know your grandfather doesn't have a shadow? He was standing outside in the sun, and I saw—*nothing*. Creepy."

Isabel's fingers stopped moving. She looked shocked. "He *used* to have one. Do you think it's hereditary? Do you think that's why *my* shadow is loose?"

Cully frowned, resting both hands on a rung of the ladder. "You said one day he just suddenly started being grumpy and mean to you, right?"

Isabel cocked her head to one side, thinking. "Grandpa has always been a bit grouchy, but he was never mean like he is now. But oh, my gosh!" She lurched slightly on the ladder, and Cully put out a hand to keep her steady. "Do you think Grandpa's so mean because he lost his shadow? Maybe he doesn't really hate me after all!"

"Hey, you two," Miggs called over. "Less talk, more work."

"Scooter says losing a shadow does different things to

different people," said Cully, thinking hard as he pulled off a little apple. "A shadow is where the not-so-good parts of a person hang out most of the time, so if you don't have one all your bad qualities have no place to go. They take you over." Cully paused, letting the idea sink in. Then he added, "So that explains a lot about your grandfather."

Isabel frowned. "I hated knowing Grandpa was stealing old people's shadows, but then when I found out he's been stealing kids' shadows, too, it made me feel so terrible. But not having a shadow!" Isabel looked at Cully with wide eyes and then rested her forehead against a rung and closed her eyes. "I wish I didn't have a loose shadow," she said. "I mean, what if when I grow up I lose it somehow, and I turn out to be rotten, just like Grandpa?"

"It could be worse," said Cully, trying to think of something comforting to say. "At least your shadow isn't frozen."

"What do you mean, *frozen*?" Isabel asked.

Cully told her about Bobo's shadow.

Isabel climbed down the ladder. She wiped her hands on her overalls and said, "I want to read about this." She picked up the book from where it had been leaning against the base of the tree. Cully climbed down, too, and the two of them sat on the grass again while Isabel looked at the table of contents.

"'Frozen Shadows, Page 32,'" Isabel read out loud. "'Frozen, rigid, stagnant, at a standstill, immobile. Interchangeable terms for when a shadow does not move in accordance with its owner. Causes are multiple, but not fully understood. This is recognized by experts in the field as being highly dangerous. Subjects are capable of extreme and unscrupulous cruelty. They are able to exert control over others, and they rarely feel remorse.'"

Isabel stopped reading and put the book down. "I bet Bobo took Grandpa's shadow," she said in a small voice.

"I bet he did, too," said Cully.

"And I bet it was because he wanted to make Grandpa steal young shadows so he could get the money for them."

"Yeah."

"I bet he even made Kipper bring old people into the store and talk them into buying cottages at Apple Blossom Acres." Isabel sighed. "Kipper just isn't smart enough to have thought that up by herself. It's weird, but knowing about Bobo actually makes me feel better about Kipper. I mean, she *is* my aunt. She kind of *tried*, you know, like taking me in when my parents died. She always made sure I had things, and provided all those lessons for me. Bobo, though—" Isabel shuddered. "You know what? I can admit something I've never said out loud before." She pulled up a few blades of grass, and in a low voice that was almost a whisper she said, "He always scared me."

"I can see why," said Cully. "Just thinking about him makes me wish Dad's shadow was in a different bank and that it didn't take two or three days for the mothballs to work."

"And I wish," Isabel went on, "that we could put some mothballs in the back room. If by some chance Grandpa's shadow is back there, we could make it remigrate."

As Cully and Isabel sat under the tree thinking, the two golden retrievers loped over to them, tongues hanging out. "Hey, dogs," said Isabel, petting first Sheba and then Shep. "I'm not afraid of them anymore, isn't that good?"

Cully nodded and, patting Shep, noticed that the dog's collar was frayed and about to break. "Hey, Shep, what have you done to—" He broke off and turned to Isabel, grinning broadly. "I just got an idea. Didn't you tell me you were good at sewing?"

"I am, I'm really great—" Isabel clapped a hand over her mouth. "Sorry, I'm trying not to brag anymore. Mrs. Towsley and I had a long talk when I was at her place, and I told her about all my troubles with the Girls. She said I should be careful not to brag about things."

Cully hugged Shep, suddenly elated. "How good do you think you'd be at sewing shadows? Just a small job."

"How small are you talking about?" Isabel asked uncertainly.

"No bigger than a dog collar." Cully cupped his hands around Shep's neck. "And hollow inside, just big enough for mothballs."

Isabel grinned. "I get it!" she squealed. "But where do we get the shadows and the moth thread?"

"Scooter told me that when you make a spy-cloak you have to cut away the head and arms and legs of the original shadow with some kind of laser beam. Scooter still has some scraps and some thread—he showed me."

"Oooh," Isabel shivered. "That's creepy."

"I know," said Cully, nodding, "it's awful, but if we can rescue other people's shadows by using them, it's worth it. Scooter's away for the day, but we'll ask him as soon as he gets back. Meanwhile, Miggs won't be happy we're goofing off."

Isabel raced to climb back up her ladder. Cully was shifting his ladder, intending to move it to a new tree, when a gaggle of girls on bicycles suddenly appeared in the orchard. Shep and Sheba galloped around them, barking happily, tails wagging a mile a minute.

"Oh, good grief," said Cully, his heart sinking.

"Hey there, Cully, whatcha doin'?" Mandy called out, jumping off her bike. Karen and Tina jumped off their bikes, too, and stood looking at Cully, grinning.

Miggs came over and said briskly, "Oh good, more helpers. We'll get this job done in no time."

Miggs pulled more ladders out of the barn, assigned two girls to a tree, and instructed them in the art of culling. Cully found a tree as far away from the girls as possible, but even so, he could hear their voices, chattery as a flock of blue jays.

Mandy seemed to enjoy the activity, but Karen quickly lost interest, preferring to play on the ground with the dogs. Tina worked in bursts of energy, climbing up a ladder and culling for a few minutes, then coming back down and lying flat on her back. Miggs came over and suggested to Karen and Tina that they dig up dandelions. "The dandelions distract the bees away from the apple blossoms," Miggs said, "so you'll be doing us a favor." Karen and Tina liked digging up dandelions, and then Shep and Sheba barked their happy barks, and there was Sam riding into the orchard on his bike.

After two hours Miggs brought everyone up to sit on the porch for lemonade and ice cream and a huge bowl of strawberries from the garden. "You worked hard," she said, "so here's your payment."

"Oh my Henry!" Mandy suddenly screamed. "It's *you*, Isabel! I didn't recognize you! I thought you were part of the family!"

Isabel, who had been bringing a spoonful of ice cream up to her mouth, put the spoon down. She opened her mouth to say something and then changed her mind.

"She *is* part of the family," said Miggs, and it was the oddest thing—all the girls were staring at Isabel, but Cully could tell they didn't hate her anymore.

Miggs set up a volleyball net. By the time the girls finally gathered up their bikes to leave and said, "Thanks, Miss Pennyacre, that was so much fun," Cully was almost sorry to see them go.

After they left, Cully and Sam and Isabel sat side by side on the swing seat looking though *Shadows and their Properties.*

"'In most, after the age of twelve, *umbrosity* gives away to *numbrosity,*'" Isabel read. "'The shadow's bonds are now subject to many influences and may become less stable.' *Numbrosity*—that's what I have, and it sounds like *numb*," she added in a depressed tone of voice.

"Go on," said Sam. "Keep reading."

"'*Numbrosity* used rarely to be seen in children under the age of twelve, but these cases seem to be on the rise. Weak bonds in children under twelve are caused by neglect, pressure, or over-indulgence.'"

"What does *that* mean?" Cully asked.

"When people buy you stuff you don't need," Isabel said, frowning. "I'm taking that dumb bike back tomorrow."

"But look at this," said Cully, pointing to the page. "'Weak bonds can be strengthened by children who stand up for themselves.' That's what you've been doing, right?"

"Yeah. I'm not going back home, you know," said Isabel.

"Not ever?"

"Not until Grandpa stops messing around with people's shadows. Not until Kipper quits trying to swipe your land." Isabel raised her small chin in the air.

"'Weak bonds can also be made stronger when an older person whose shadow is firmly bonded takes an interest in the young person,'" Cully read.

Isabel beamed. "That's good old Mrs. Towsley they're talking about. She's taking an interest in me, and I found out her shadow can't be separated. She just made it look like it was that day at Batty's. Some old trick she learned."

The porch railings made a shadowy grid on the porch floor. Isabel got up from the swing seat and stood in a square of sunlight and looked at her shadow. "Think my shadow is attached better than it was?"

"I think your shadow *might* seem darker," Cully said, staring hard at it.

"Yeah, sure," said Sam cheerfully. "Darker and, I don't know, *stronger.*"

Cully smiled, but he thought Isabel *was* different from the girl who had recited that endless poem on the school stage only a few months ago. Then he remembered that Inca had suggested Isabel be invited over to help out with the Recipe. The more poems the better, she had said. "Say, Isabel, do you still know that poem you memorized for Peebles?"

"'The Ballad of Sam McGee,'" said Isabel. She took a deep breath and opened her mouth.

"You don't have to say it right now," said Cully hurriedly. "But we're having a party here the day after tomorrow—a bonfire and a cookout—and we're each going to recite a poem—and we want you to come."

"Peaches and cream!" Isabel exclaimed. "I've never been invited to a party by anyone before."

Sam scowled. "What kind of a dumb party is that?" he asked. "I mean, where you recite *poetry?*"

Cully turned to him. "You're coming, Sam, and you have to learn a poem, too."

"Me?" Sam looked alarmed.

"I'll coach you," said Isabel, looking even more pleased.

14

Two days later Cully went with Opal into town to help her buy food for the cookout. Opal wanted to stop at the bank first, and as Cully stood with her waiting in line for a teller he was able to see Bobo Ballou through the window of his office—there he was, sitting there with his frozen shadow. What had the book said? *Subjects are capable of extreme and unscrupulous cruelty. They are able to exert control over others, and they rarely feel remorse.*

Panicky suddenly, Cully turned to Opal. "While you're waiting, I just want to go and check on something."

Cully found the clerk who had the key to the safe-deposit box. She waited outside the vault again as Cully opened the box. The treasure box was there, next to the envelope. He pulled out the envelope with a trembling hand, opened it, and peered in. The shadow was gone.

Cully stood there wishing he could be happy about this, but he didn't know what it meant: either his father's shadow had remigrated, or it had been stolen by Bobo Ballou before the naphthalene ever had a chance to work.

Cully thanked the clerk and ran upstairs. Opal was finally standing at the teller's window, writing out a check. "Oh drat," she burst out, "I just signed my name 'Edna St. Vincent Millay.'" She tore up the check and wrote a new one. "One way or another, I'll be glad when this day is over."

Cully looked at her in amazement. "You went and memorized a poem by Edna St. Vincent Millay," he said. Just like Miggs, Opal had been saying over and over again that the poetry part of the Recipe was nonsense.

"I won second place at Peebles when I was in eighth grade," said Opal, blushing slightly. "I like memorizing poetry."

"But you don't really think the Recipe is going to work, do you, Opal?" he asked.

Opal gazed thoughtfully at Cully. "No," she said, "but I want it to."

She couldn't have expressed his own feelings better.

When they arrived home Cully helped Miggs in the orchard for a few hours, then he slipped back into town to Mrs. Towlsey's apartment. It was situated over the candy and newspaper and magazine store. When Mrs. Towsley came to the door, Fitz rushed past her, almost knocking Cully over with little yelps of joy. "Okay, boy," Cully said, kneeling and throwing his arms around him. "I'm happy to see you, too."

"I guess he knows a friend when he sees one," said Mrs. Towsley, smiling.

Cully looked up at the small, bird-like woman. Isabel had been right. Mrs. Towsley didn't look like a person who had lost her shadow, and anyway he could see it stretching into the hallway.

"I'd like to take Fitz back to Batty now," he said.

Mrs. Towsley cocked her head at Cully. "You'd take him back there, would you?"

"Got my reasons," said Cully.

Mrs. Towsley wagged a finger at Cully fiercely. "Now listen here, young man, you don't want to be mixed up with the likes of Jim Bates."

Cully shook his head. "I'm not mixed up with him. I *was* working for him, but he fired me. I would have quit anyhow."

"That is a mighty good thing," Mrs. Towsley said, somewhat less sternly, "but young man, you watch your back when you're around him, and no—no questions—that's all I'm going to say for now."

Cully didn't have a leash with him, but he didn't need one. Fitz trotted right beside Cully, pressing so close to his legs it was difficult to walk. As they approached the store, Fitz slowed down and began to growl. Cully paused and knelt again, talking to the dog face-to-face. "Now listen up, Fitzy-Fitz, I know you're mad at your master, but as far as I can tell he's never done you any harm. In fact you may be the only one he really loves. So go in there like a man—I mean, like a dog—'cause you have an important job to do."

Fitz licked Cully's face, and Cully stood up and pulled the shadow collar out of his pocket.

"I got you a new collar, Fitz." Cully slipped the new one over the old one. "Blends right in. Now, no biting when you get in there, and you gotta pretend to like the guy."

Cully walked into the store. Batty was up on his perch.

"What are you doing here?" Batty snapped. "I fired you."

"I brought Fitz back," said Cully.

Batty's eyes bulged. "You brought back Fitz?"

Batty climbed down from his stool and slowly came out from behind the counter.

"But take it easy," Cully cautioned as Batty moved toward Fitz. "He needs time to get used to you again. Don't raise your voice, and don't get too close for a while. Like for at least a week. You gave him a pretty bad shock, yelling at Isabel like that."

Batty stopped in his tracks as Fitz growled. "Yes, yes, of course, you're right. Good boy, you're a good boy!" he said crooningly. "The most satisfactory of all quadrupeds." He cleared his throat awkwardly. "How is Isabel? Is she all right?" For a moment his face creased with anxiety. "Tell her—tell her—oh, I don't know." Fitz went over to his corner and lay down. "Does me good to see Fitz back here," said Batty gruffly. "Been kind of lonely since—well, since everything happened." Batty placed a hand against his chest. "You, Isabel, and Fitz—all embers in the furnace of my heart, extinguished in one day."

"Gotta go now," said Cully.

"You were a good apprentice," said Batty, smiling just enough to reveal his broken tooth. "Too bad about everything."

"Yeah," said Cully on his way to the door. He thought about his great-grandfather Cullen's watch. He didn't think he'd ever get it back now. He bent down and kissed Fitz on the nose, catching a whiff of the mothballs. They smelled as beautiful to him as perfume, and he hoped they'd be a thousand times more useful.

As evening approached, the sky kept filling with clouds.

"Not sure Inca's going to get her full moon," said Miggs, looking up. She was busy making up hamburger patties for the cookout.

Miggs had agreed to help cook for the cookout, and with her science background had shown an interest in the Recipe. But she was drawing the line at learning a poem. "No truck I know of," she had said, "is going to run on poetry."

Sam arrived. "Let's go reel in some fresh fish for tonight," he said. Cully had no idea whether or not Sam had learned a poem. Every time Cully asked him, Sam shrugged, saying, "Workin' on it."

The two boys headed with the dogs down the path to the river. Something about the quality of the light, the freshness of the air, the companionship of the dogs reminded Cully of countless evenings he had sat by the river, fishing with his father. At the riverbank now, Cully knelt and threw an arm around each dog. "Is the Recipe going to work?" he whispered in Shep's ear.

Shep gave him a sloppy dog kiss.

"But I'm not going to think about tonight," Cully said to Sheba. Sheba poked her nose against his face as if in agreement.

But as Cully sat with his fishing rod in hand, the birches along the bank cast white lines on the black water. The opening lines of the poem he had memorized—*When I see birches bend to left and right across the line of darker trees*—sprang automatically into his mind.

"I'm worried Leapin' Lizzie won't like my poem," Cully said to Sam. "I should have learned one about engines."

"Now I know you're just as crazy as the rest of your family," said Sam good-naturedly.

Cully relaxed. Sam thought it was all a game, and maybe that's all, in the end, it was—the whole family was playing a game as a way of distracting themselves from worry.

Shep and Sheba started barking, but their tails were wagging. "Uh-oh, there goes our peace and quiet," said Sam as Isabel came running down the path. She was wearing a yellow T-shirt and the same pair of overalls she had worn the day before. It seemed to Cully that she had molted like a lizard, and shed the color pink.

"I've got some news," Isabel shouted. The dogs converged on her, and she didn't mind.

"Shh," said Sam, turning on her. "You'll scare the fish."

Isabel scowled, but she settled down on the bank with the dogs beside her. She sat very still, and soon the only movement was the flicking of the dogs' ears or the skimming of water striders on the surface of the river.

"I got one! I got one!" Sam yelled.

An hour later Cully and Sam had caught five fish between them.

"You brought us good luck," said Sam to Isabel. "I didn't think a girl could keep so still or so quiet."

"Can I talk now?" Isabel asked, but she didn't wait for permission. "I was down by the river," she said, the words tumbling rapidly out of her. "Along that part where the Masumotos have their cabin, and Cully, I think I saw your dad."

Cully froze, staring at her.

"I didn't get a real good view because he was going into the cabin. He was with Mr. Masumoto's son."

"His *son*? Kento is supposed to be in Japan." Even as he said it, Cully thought of the birthday postcard his father had sent with the Japanese silkworm laborers on it. Maybe Kento and his father had run into each other, and—

"Well, Kento *was* down by the river, I'm sure of that," said Isabel. "And there was a guy with him, and I thought he looked like your dad. Don't you see, Cully?" Isabel gave a little skip of excitement. "The naphthalene must have worked, and your father got his shadow back, and now he's home!"

"I checked on the envelope at the bank this morning, and it was empty," said Cully slowly. His heart was pounding, and he felt slightly dizzy. "But why would Dad be staying with the Masumotos instead of coming here?"

Sam shook his head. "It doesn't make sense," he said. "Are you absolutely sure it was Cully's dad, Isabel?"

Isabel tugged on a strand of hair. "I don't know," she said finally. "Now I—I'm not totally sure."

Cully and Sam stared at Isabel in dismay.

"I'm—I'm sorry," Isabel said. She scuffed at the ground with the heel of one sneaker. "Now I think it was someone else."

"You shouldn't have said anything unless you were sure," Sam said, frowning at her.

Sam started down the path to the house. Isabel hung back, turning to Cully. "I'm sorry," she said again. Cully kept his mouth clamped shut. He was too disappointed to trust himself to say anything comforting to Isabel. He had felt, just for a moment, as if he'd caught the best fish in the world, only to see that fish slip off the hook and swim away. Shep raced ahead but Sheba stayed back, close to Cully, as if she knew he was upset.

As Sam, Isabel, and Cully climbed up the stairs to the middle floor, the smell of Opal's rhubarb-strawberry pie filled the entire house and lifted Cully's spirits. Isabel's words haunted Cully. What if she *had* seen his father? First chance he got, Cully was going over to the Masumotos'.

"Isn't this fun?" asked Inca as family and guests finally sat down around the picnic table. "And this early summer evening air is so soft," she added dreamily.

"Mosquitoes like it," said Miggs matter-of-factly, lighting candles that were supposed to keep the bugs away.

"This is the best food ever," said Scooter, rubbing his stomach many helpings later. "I see there are a couple of pies, too."

"I think we should save dessert," said Inca. "It's time we got started. There's the moon." Everyone turned to look, and saw the moon rising like a balloon above the trees.

Cully and Sam helped Scooter wrestle a barrel of apple fuel over to Leapin' Lizzie.

Scooter bent down and, turning a spigot in the barrel, filled a brand-new canister with the apple fuel. It had a flexible hose that bent into Leapin Lizzie's tank.

"Time for the spotlight," said Miggs. In spite of her skepticism, she had climbed up into Jack's maple tree earlier in the day and tied a lamp to its branches so it would shine down on the truck. She had even placed stumps around for people to sit on. "So let's get started," she said, "and get this over with."

"Youngest to oldest?" asked Inca. "Or oldest to youngest?"

"I'll begin," said Opal.

Opal clasped her hands together in front of her like an old-fashioned schoolgirl and began. " 'God's World,' by Edna St. Vincent Millay." Her voice was strained and more high-pitched than usual. "*O World, I cannot hold thee close* enough! / *Thy winds, thy wide, grey skies / Thy mists that roll and rise!*"

Cully felt a rush of love for his serious aunt. The tree frogs piped up in the momentary silence that followed when she finished, and then everyone clapped heartily. Opal's pale face was flushed.

"Scooter, you're up," said Inca.

Scooter rose to his feet. "'Casey at the Bat,' by Ernest Thayer," he said woodenly. He cleared his throat and launched into his poem as if he were gunning the engine to beat a red light. Cully carefully avoided looking at Sam. It would be terrible to burst out laughing. Halfway through, Scooter suddenly halted. Inca, next to him, murmured a few words, and Scooter got going again.

"*But there is no joy in Mudville—mighty Casey has struck out*," Scooter said slowly and sadly at the end.

"That was wonderful, Scooter," said Inca enthusiastically as everyone else clapped and cheered.

"It's your turn now, Inca," said Scooter gruffly.

Inca began. "'My Shadow,' by Robert Louis Stevenson."

Cully felt a shiver up the back of his neck as Inca's voice, light and clear, carried effortlessly: "*I have a little shadow that goes in and out with me...*" How like Inca to choose a child's poem about shadows—and seeing all the shadows, distinctly visible in the spotlight, filled Cully with relief. He was glad every single person around him had one.

"Let's take a short break and have our pie," said Opal when everyone had clapped for Inca. "An intermission between the older generation and the younger."

The mood was cheerful as everyone left their spots by the truck.

"We should do this every full moon," said Miggs. "Just leave out Leapin' Lizzie's part in it."

"Opal, this pie has to be one of your best!" said Inca. "And now," Inca said as Scooter devoured his third helping, "Act Two."

As everyone gathered once more in front of the truck, Sam stood up. "'The Wreck of the Hesperus,' by Henry Wadsworth Longfellow."

Cully listened in amazement as Sam galloped through all twenty-two verses, his cheerful face beaming in the firelight. He was obviously enjoying himself. There was a huge cheer when he finished.

"I could have listened to that forever!" Opal exclaimed.

"Your turn, Cully," said Inca.

Cully's throat felt tight. He realized he wanted the Recipe to work more than he'd been willing to admit.

"Cully?"

That was Inca, prodding him.

Cully clenched his hands into fists and closed his eyes. "'Birches,'" he said, "by Robert Frost."

As he recited, Cully saw himself walking around the farm with his father after an ice storm, inspecting all the destruction the storm had caused—the downed telephone and electric lines, the snapped tops of pine trees, and, yes, bent birches; and yet "It's so magical," his father had said— and it had been, with rainbows winking through ice crystals as the sun shone, and everything quieter than usual except for that "click of branch on branch."

Cully was getting through the poem. He was reciting, "*Earth's the right place for love*," when he was conscious of a movement behind him. His eyes flew open, and a shadowy form just outside the ring of light coalesced out of the darkness—a tall, looming, shadowy shape. It flowed toward Cully, and he suddenly felt enveloped by a sensation of warmth and comfort. He was unable to go on with the poem.

"Cully?"

Cully saw Sam staring at him. Cully forced himself to pick up where he had left off, and when he finished with "*One could do worse than be a swinger of birches*" the others clapped and cheered. But Cully was barely conscious of the applause. He kept peering into the shadows, wondering what he had seen.

"Isabel's turn," said Sam.

Before she launched into the poem, Isabel stood with her arms tightly folded against her chest. "I dedicate this to Grandpa," Isabel said in a thin, tight voice. " 'Cause he helped me learn this before—before he—" She swallowed hard, and then she was off and running. " 'The Ballad of Sam McGee,' " she said, "by Robert W. Service. '*There are strange things done in the midnight sun / By the men who moil for gold…*' "

Isabel was just as dramatic as she had been at the Peebles contest, perhaps even more so because she had an audience now that appreciated her. Everyone stood at the end when she finished. "Bravo, Isabel!" they shouted, and Isabel's face glowed.

"If the Recipe doesn't work after this," said Inca, "it never will."

Scooter opened the door to the truck and was about to climb in behind the wheel when a red convertible spun into the driveway, shattering the festive mood.

"Oh no," Opal groaned as Bobo and Kipper and Batty

climbed out. The dogs flung themselves at the intruders in a frenzy of barking.

"Oh, Isabel, you *are* here," Kipper cried out. She hung back slightly, afraid of the dogs.

"You're coming home, Isabel," Bobo said, barging past the dogs. He looked enormous and menacing in the moonlight.

"No," said Isabel. "I'm not."

"Yes," said Bobo, walking toward her, "you are. Right now."

"You can't make me." Isabel's voice quavered, and Miggs and the barking dogs placed themselves firmly between Isabel and the approaching Ballous.

Bobo held up an envelope and turned his attention to Cully. "Marble collection, eh?" he snarled, taking a step toward Cully. His eyes were stone cold. "Never knew marbles were made out of naphthalene. Nice try, but I'm afraid you didn't try hard enough." Cully's heart sank. "When Isabel comes home," Bobo said, "I will *consider* returning the contents of this envelope to you."

"I'll come," said Isabel, but Shep and Sheba pressed close to her, growling, and they wouldn't let her move.

"Don't, Isabel," said Cully. "You can't trust him to keep his word."

And then the memory of that dark warmth that had briefly overtaken him as he finished his poem came back to Cully. His father's shadow might very well be in the envelope Bobo was holding, but it was also true that Bobo might be bluffing. There was only one way to be sure. Heart pounding, he drew in a breath and positioned himself to spring.

"Wait." Batty stepped forward. Until now he had been partially concealed in the shadows. "Maybe—maybe we ought to be *asking* her. Isabel, I mean." He looked wan and pitiful in the moonlight, and his voice was thin and hoarse. "Isabel," he said, reaching a shaking hand toward her, "do you want to come home?"

Bobo and Kipper snapped around to stare at him. "What are you talking about?" Bobo asked harshly. "It was your idea to come here and—wait a minute—" He broke off, staring, and pointed. "Look at his shadow, it's—"

But Bobo broke off again because Cully lunged and grabbed the envelope and then ran for Leapin' Lizzie. He threw himself behind the wheel, pressed his foot down on the clutch, and turned the key in the ignition. Cully heard yelling, but he also heard the sound of the engine combusting. Leapin' Lizzie leaped into action. Cully pulled the door shut and lurched out of the driveway.

Out on Route 5 Cully got the truck into second gear, and then third, and then headed for the open road.

15

Cully's heart was hammering. He wanted to pick up the envelope and look in it, but he could hear the engine of the red convertible roaring behind him and see it in the rearview mirror. He gingerly pressed down harder on the accelerator, not knowing how fast he could go and still keep control. White-knuckled, he gripped the steering wheel, commanding himself to keep his eyes on the road and not be tempted to look back over his shoulder.

River Road was coming up—the winding dirt road that led to the Masumoto cabin, where Isabel said she thought she had seen Jack. Cully knew the road was in bad shape—he had been down it recently with Sam and his father in their Jeep. He spun the wheel to the right, fervently hoping the little red sports car wouldn't be able to handle the deep ruts.

The truck rattled along, jouncing and bouncing. The moon shone down on the cornfields to the left and right, on the potato and strawberry farms, on pastures and silos and wooden fences.

All at once it struck Cully that the moon and the poetry had worked! Leapin' Lizzie was leaping, all right!

Now the road, turning left, ran alongside the river. Cully passed a shabby-looking shack perched on the bank. It was the Stickses' place. An old weathered dock, a few of its boards missing, came into view. A little farther along Cully came to the small, neat cabin belonging to the Masumoto family. He passed their garden, and then their dock, and saw two aluminum canoes turned upside down on it.

The red car was still following him. With a sinking heart, Cully realized Bobo would keep following him until he ran out of fuel—or worse, overtake him on this mostly deserted stretch of road. Cully slammed on the brakes and turned off the engine. He grabbed the envelope off the seat and threw himself out of the truck. He ran full steam toward the dock.

The red car screeched into a ditch beside the road. Stuffing the envelope into his pocket, Cully turned over a canoe and dragged it to the edge of the dock.

"You little squirt," Bobo shouted, panting as he stormed onto the dock. He reached out and gripped Cully's arm hard, his face red and furious in the moonlight. "How did you do it?" he asked.

"How did I—?"

"How did you restore Batty? I was keeping his shadow at my house, so you must have gotten your hands on it somehow. Did that little sneak Isabel give it to you? If she did, I'm going to—"

"Isabel didn't have anything to do with it," Cully said, "and neither did I." Wrenching free of Bobo's grasp, Cully shoved the canoe into the water and flung himself into it. He landed hard in the bottom as Bobo, lunging to grab him, lost his balance, and fell half in the canoe, half in the water. The craft tilted sharply and began to take on water rapidly. Bobo floundered for a second before the current caught him, and then he was sent swirling downstream. Cully, clutching on to the half-submerged canoe, went swirling after him.

The current was strong and the water was cold. Gasping, Cully lost hold of the canoe; he sank once, and then again. In mounting panic he flailed and kicked and thrashed, trying desperately to keep his head above the water.

And then Cully remembered: *If you fall overboard, don't fight the current; just try to float.* His father had said those very words on their last canoe trip.

Cully rolled over onto his back, stretched out his arms, and forced his feet to float up. The sky spun dizzily above him, and trees along the bank rushed by. This was better, and he relaxed slightly as he bobbed downstream like any piece of flotsam caught in the current. But he wasn't a piece of wood, and he couldn't float forever. His neck ached from the strain of keeping his head up, and his limbs were beginning to feel dangerously heavy. If only he had something to hold on to—but then, oddly, he stopped moving, even though the water continued to rush by.

Sitting up slowly, Cully saw he had come to rest in the middle of the river; he was on a patch of mud where broken tree trunks poked up eerily in the moonlight. He sat motionless, trying to catch his breath. With numb fingers he groped for the envelope in his pocket. It was gone.

Cully pulled up his knees and rested his head wearily against them, his thoughts swirling like the river itself. What if Jack's shadow had been in the envelope? Could a shadow withstand a soaking, or might it be sucked down into a whirlpool, never to be seen again? Or what if his father *had* returned from Japan, and his shadow had come back to him? Even with a shadow, how good was it going to be for Jack to have to face the fact that Pennyacre Farm was soon to be cut up into lots for storage sheds?

But then something glinting upstream in the moonlight caught Cully's eye. He slowly lifted his head. An aluminum canoe was swiftly plowing through the white water. One lone paddler was leaning forward, straining to navigate the swift water, and before long the canoe reached the mud patch. The tall, broad frame of a man stood out clearly as he made his way over the mud.

"Here we go," said Jack, bending down to haul Cully to his feet. Cully was trembling from head to toe—he didn't know if his father was real or an apparition, and his legs simply wouldn't work. Cully was scooped up around the middle, and in a moment he was sitting in the canoe, out on the river again, moving in a diagonal line across the current for the shore. At last the canoe crunched up onto a rocky beach.

Jack rested the paddle on his knees for a moment, sweat pouring down his face, and then he climbed out.

"Here," he said, holding his hand out to Cully. Cully saw his father's shadow stretching bumpily over the rocky shore.

"Dad," Cully said, his voice cracking. He was shivering violently now.

Jack put his arms around Cully, and for the second time that night Cully was flooded with the sensation of warmth and comfort, but this time it was accompanied by solid flesh and bones.

What followed was dreamlike: a walk along the river until they came to the Masumoto cabin. Warm, dry clothes were provided by Kento Masumoto. As Cully and Jack sat at a table drinking hot tea brewed by Mrs. Masumoto, Cully described his struggle with Bobo Ballou and how he had last seen him being swept downriver by the current. Mrs. Masumoto went to the phone and called the police. Then Kento explained how he had found Jack working on a silkworm farm in Japan. But Jack hadn't seemed like the man Kento remembered, and, concerned, Kento had managed to bring him back to Medley.

"But I didn't want to go home to the farm," Jack said, running a hand across his face. "I don't know why. I was— not myself—"

"It was because of the shadow-thief," said Mrs. Masumoto. She folded her hands across her chest, looking somber.

"I don't understand," said Jack.

"My shadow came back yesterday," said Mr. Masumoto. He was sitting at the table, beaming, nodding his head, and his shadow's head nodded with him.

Mrs. Masumoto pointed to Jack's shadow. "And his, too, you see? Just about an hour ago, it came back. We saw the change."

About an hour ago, Cully figured, they were all still reciting their poems. But now Jack was waving his hands in the air, watching his shadow hands wave with him.

"Shadow-thief," Jack said slowly, and then his face cleared. "Of course! I understand now—I understand everything! Except how and why my shadow remigrated."

"Mothballs," Cully said tentatively.

"Naphthalene," said Jack, nodding. "Good for you for figuring it out."

Cully sat without saying anything more, but he was thinking about Batty's shadow, locked up at the Ballous' house. How had Batty's shadow been returned to *him*?

"Look at that!" Jack exclaimed when he saw Leapin' Lizzie. "You got the Recipe to work!"

Cully nodded as he climbed into the truck on the passenger side. He was only too happy to let his father drive. He was glad, too, as they drove away, to see the last of the red car as it sat abandoned on the side of the road. He wondered what sort of shape Bobo would be in when the police finally found him.

"It is so grand to be home," Jack said as the landscape drifted by. "Been all over the world, and nothing I've seen is as beautiful as this."

Cully was pressed as close to his father as he could get. "Are you staying now, Dad?" he asked.

Jack put an arm around Cully and held him close. "Not ever leaving again," he said.

As Leapin' Lizzie rattled up the driveway, the family burst out of the farmhouse. And then there was pandemonium. Shep and Sheba ran in circles, tails wagging, barking like crazy. Inca cried, "Jack! Jack!" over and over again. Opal wrung her hands, and Miggs stared up at the moon fiercely as if she didn't know what else to do.

Scooter hung back, watching shyly, and Isabel stood close to Batty. Cully saw clearly the smudge of gray shadow Batty cast in the driveway. It was an odd coincidence, he thought, both Batty's and his father's shadows returning at the same time.

Opal was leading them all back into the house when a

police car came roaring up the driveway, blue lights blazing. A sturdy, official-looking man climbed out of one side of the car and Leona Towsley out of the other.

"We're looking for James Bates," the man said, flashing an ID. "We're from AASC. Agency Against Shadow Collectors."

"James Bates, you are under arrest for collecting AOLFs, or Absence of Light Forms," Mrs. Towsley said, also flashing an ID. Both she and the officer marched toward Batty.

"No," Isabel said in a wail.

"I'm afraid it's the right thing to do, Isabel," Mrs. Towsley said quietly. "We've had our eye on your grandfather for a long time now, and there is no question he violated the terms of the Versailles Peace Treaty as defined in Section 3792. He has also been collecting the AOLFs of juveniles, a more serious violation—and that gives our agency even more authority to take him in."

"But he didn't mean to do all that bad stuff," said Isabel. "It was because he lost his shadow—he has it back now—he won't do it anymore."

Batty collapsed against Isabel for a moment. "The only good thing I ever did, Isabel, was keep you out of the store as much as possible and not take your shadow when I had plenty of opportunity to do so." Batty took off his glasses and wiped his eyes.

"It's time to go, Mr. Bates," said Mrs. Towsley. The officer took a step toward Batty, holding out a pair of handcuffs.

"No, Grandpa, you can't go," said Isabel, clutching Batty's arm.

Batty gently disentangled himself from Isabel. "Isabel, take good care of Fitz. Leona Towsley, take good care of my granddaughter. And Isabel Ballou, I always loved you, even when I didn't have a shadow." He kissed Isabel, the officer secured his wrists, and he was gone.

16

Several afternoons later the Pennyacres were sitting on the porch. Much to everyone's relief, Scooter was there, too. AASC had come investigating him, and Dwayne Sticks, too, but as neither man had worked long in the shadow business, and both had quit their jobs (Dwayne quit the moment Archie's shadow remigrated), AASC settled on putting both men on probation and keeping an eye on their activities for a year.

The police found Bobo half-drowned and washed up in a cove in a bend of the river, and he was taken almost directly to jail. Kipper had been apprehended, too, and she was going to have to pay back all the people whose money she had taken. Mrs. Towsley was officially taking care of Isabel and Fitz—for how long, no one knew, but Cully knew that Isabel secretly hoped it would be forever.

Now the family was telling Jack about Batty and Kipper and Bobo and Apple Blossom Acres.

"Isn't that terrible?" asked Inca at the end of the story.

Jack leaped to his feet, throwing up his arms. "Jumping Jehoshaphat!" he shouted. "*We* should build cottages! Cully and I, that is. And then we can rent them, and I'll be the caretaker. I can't think of a more perfect job for me, and don't you see? The income will get us through the hard times."

"Well," said Miggs after the long silence that followed. "That's a dandy idea as long as you don't suddenly decide to go off and seek your fortune again." Her tone was slightly sarcastic, and Cully knew it would take some time before she stopped being mad at Jack.

"If I hadn't lost my shadow, you *know* I never would have left," said Jack.

Miggs answered with a slight humph.

"But *how* did you lose it?" Cully asked.

Jack shuddered, remembering. "It came back to me the other night—the whole scene. I told Batty I knew he was collecting shadows, and shortly after that he invited me back into the studio. To my surprise Bobo Ballou was there. Before I could do anything, Bobo took a swing at me—knocked me out—and when I came to, I was lying on the floor of that studio. I realize now that's when Batty must have collected my shadow." Jack spoke haltingly, a haunted look in his eyes. "And then not long after that, Bobo must have stripped Batty of *his* shadow." He shuddered again, and no one said anything for a while.

Scooter broke the silence. "I'd like to help build the cottages," he said shyly. "I'm a good carpenter."

"We can build one for Mr. Crimps and one for Kento Masumoto," said Cully, getting excited, "and one for Isabel and Mrs. Towsley and Fitz—"

"—and one—one for Scooter and me," Inca burst in, "because we're getting married!" Her copper hair flowed over her shoulders, and her eyes were shining. "And," she added, "guess what? I finished *Mothology*! My publisher loves it! He gave me a huge advance, and we can pay this month's mortgage."

"Oh!" said Opal with a gasp.

"And Opal," Inca went on, "I went out and bought you a new blouse. It's time you wore some bright colors."

Inca pulled a bright blue blouse out of a bag she was holding and went over and held it up against Opal, who suddenly looked dazzling.

Everyone leaped up and hugged Inca and slapped Scooter heartily on the back—everyone, that is, except for Cully, who felt overwhelmed. He liked Scooter, and he was happy for Inca, but it made her seem different...so... grown-up. He sat rooted to the swing seat, just watching all the commotion.

When all the congratulating had died down, Inca said, "But what about the Recipe? We're not giving up on that, are we? You were right about what was needed to make it work, Jack."

"What on earth are you talking about?" asked Jack.

"You know as well as I do," said Inca. "The key to the Recipe: you have to memorize a poem and recite it under a full moon. Really—who would have guessed? But what a success!"

Jack stared at her. "Good gravy, Inca, reciting the poem under a full moon has nothing to do with the Recipe! The poetry-moon thing is a method one uses to get shadows to remigrate—a virtually unknown method," he added, looking around nervously, and then he smiled wryly. "I don't know why I feel as if I have to keep it a secret from all of you—you know more about shadows than I do at this point."

"Remigrate?" Opal asked.

Jack leaned forward, explaining. "You wait for a full moon, and then you think about the person whose shadow you're trying to get to return—I mean, *really* think—and then you recite a poem."

Cully thought of the dark form that had materialized as he finished reciting his poem, and the feeling of warmth that had washed over him. Everything clicked into place. "That must be how we got your shadow back, Dad!" he exclaimed. "We memorized poems and recited them under the full moon—" He shuddered, thinking what a close call it had all been. It meant, of course, that Bobo Ballou had taken Jack's shadow out of the envelope before the mothballs could do their work. He had arrived at the Pennyacres' believing the shadow was in that envelope, because it very likely had been when he set out. "And Batty's shadow," Cully added slowly, "must have remigrated when Isabel recited *her* poem."

Cully shuddered again as he thought about Bobo—what, he wondered, would cause a person's shadow to freeze in the first place? He'd have to remember to ask his father about that sometime—and then he couldn't help smiling. There were a million questions he could ask now, and his father was there to answer all of them.

"You mean—all that poetry-reciting actually has something to do with bringing back people's shadows?" Miggs asked.

Jack beamed. "Do you know what this means for the thousands of people all over the world who have lost their shadows?"

Miggs hooked her fingers into the straps of her overalls. "Maybe," she said thoughtfully, "I'll learn a poem by the next full moon."

"Why, Miggs," said Inca, "does that mean you actually believe—"

Inca never finished her sentence, because a green Volkswagen Bug pulled into the driveway. Shep and Sheba rushed down the porch stairs, but there was a happy lilt to their barking and their tails were wagging. The doors of the car opened and Isabel appeared, and then Mrs. Towsley. Isabel ran up onto the porch, and Mrs. Towsley followed more slowly.

"Guess what, guess what, guess what?" Isabel's voice was high-pitched with excitement. "Mrs. Towsley took me back into Grandpa's studio, and she ran a test on me. My shadow is umbrose! It won't separate! And Mrs. T. says it never will again!"

Scooter stood up and gave his chair to Mrs. Towsley. Mrs. Towsley settled into it, smiling fondly at Isabel.

"And we went to visit Grandpa in jail," Isabel went on, "and Grandpa told me to go to the store and get this for you." She pulled a silver pocket watch out of a small, flannel bag she was carrying and handed the watch to Jack. "Grandpa said this belongs to you," she said shyly.

Jack held the watch up in the air for a moment, letting it twirl by its chain. Then he handed it to Cully. "This belongs to you," he said, "and I'm not waiting until you're twenty-one to give it to you. Cullen was the Pennyacre who planted the first apple trees, and now you, Cully, are the Pennyacre who has made it possible for us to keep those trees." He paused for a moment. "I believe there's an old saying—that one can measure the worth of a man by how dark his shadow is." He pulled Cully to his feet. "See there," he said, pointing.

In the late afternoon sun, Cully's shadow did seem very dark on the wooden boards of the old porch.

"We should celebrate all the good news," said Opal, standing. "I think this occasion calls for a pie."

As Opal went into the house, Scooter hurried down the stairs and disappeared into the barn. He came back holding a sheaf of papers. "So," he said, going over to Jack, "this Recipe of yours—if it wasn't the full moon making the apple fuel work, what was it?"

Scooter pulled up another chair next to Jack's; Miggs pulled her chair over, too, and soon all three heads were bent over the diagrams. As it grew dark, Inca turned on the porch lights. Moths fluttered, and out in the orchard fireflies flickered. Cully pulled another chair as close to Jack as he could get.

That night Cully's shadow took him by the hand and led him into the shadow world. Cully was growing used to the sensation of being squished flat, and he soon found himself transformed into the familiar form of a lightow. The grainy world of shadows was illuminated by many lightows, and Cully saw that they belonged to many shadow personages, including, he realized happily, one that resembled his father in shape and size. The shadowy dogs were there, too, lying down at the base of a shadowy tree. The shadow personages gathered before the tree, and they began to sing—a sound that reminded Cully of the humming of bees—and after a moment all the lightows became suffused with a reddish-gold light.

When Cully woke up the next morning, he was filled with a lightness of being he hadn't felt for a long time.

Jack hasn't been able to find anyone to invest in the Recipe, but Scooter thinks someday someone will take an interest in it, and he shouldn't give up on it. Anyhow, there will be HUGE savings for us—for instance, it will cost us a fraction of the usual amount to heat the house and all the outbuildings, including the new cottages, and a fraction of what we usually pay to run all the vehicles and the cider press. Melvin would have gotten a real hoot out of this one. Good old Jack!

October 14, 1963

I am sitting at my desk, looking out the window of my studio. I can see some of the new cottages Jack and Cully and Scooter have finished. Inca and Scooter are happily settled in one of them. Any day now, Isabel and Fitz and Mrs. Towsley will be moving into another one. Shep and Sheba have already adopted Fitz, taking him for a dip in the river and a romp in the orchard every time he comes for a visit.

And now I can see Cully, walking toward the house from the Chicken Coop, where he and Jack are living again. Cully seems to be carrying something—oh, I can see what it is now, it's Jack's old treasure box, the one he always kept in the Mouse House.

Cully is stopping at the maple tree, and now he's bending down and picking up a handful of red leaves. The leaves that are still on the tree are standing out like flames against the sky.

Cully is carefully placing the leaves in the box—and now he is opening the little door to the Mouse House. There—the box is inside, safe and sound.